"I'm not going to stand in your way.

It would be a mistake for you to blow off this opportunity."

"What if I don't get the job?" Bryan asked.

Blackness fell over Jade's heart, which was ridiculous due to the perfect summer day. But how was she supposed to answer that? If he didn't get the job, he might be willing to explore a relationship with her?

"You've been clear all along on two things. You're moving, and you aren't dating."

He narrowed his eyes. "And you've been crystal clear that we're just friends."

"What do you want?" Jade shifted her weight to one hip. "You kissed me, knowing full well you plan on moving to Canada. I love Lake Endwell. I'm happy here. If you need to move, I get it, but I don't want to be your backup plan."

Hurt flashed in Bryan's eyes, but she couldn't, wouldn't feel guilty. She twisted, unable to face him a second longer. Her mouth tasted of copper at the thought of being his second choice.

Just once in her life, she wanted to be someone's first choice.

Jill Kemerer writes novels with love, humor and faith. Besides spoiling her minidachshund and keeping up with her busy kids, Jill reads stacks of books, lives for her morning coffee and gushes over fluffy animals. She resides in Ohio with her husband and two children. Jill loves connecting with readers, so please visit her website, jillkemerer.com, or contact her at PO Box 2802, Whitehouse, OH 43571.

Books by Jill Kemerer

Love Inspired

Small-Town Bachelor
Unexpected Family
Her Small-Town Romance

Her Small-Town Romance

Jill Kemerer

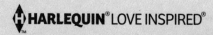

 LOVE INSPIRED BOOKS

Recycling programs
for this product may
not exist in your area.

ISBN-13: 978-0-373-71948-8

Her Small-Town Romance

Copyright © 2016 by Jill Kemerer

www.Harlequin.com

Printed in U.S.A.

When I am afraid, I put my trust in you.
—*Psalms* 56:3

To my writing team.
Shana Asaro, I'm a better writer because of
you. Rachel Kent, thank you for your friendship
and for guiding my career. Wendy Paine Miller,
you're the real deal and I treasure you.
Jessica R. Patch, for holding me up with joy
as we journey together.

Chapter One

Bryan Sheffield scanned the parking lot as he paced under the pavilion at Evergreen Park. His students, most likely retirees and a few college kids, should be arriving any minute. He had no idea how many people would show up for the free outdoor course. Ideally, ten or twelve. If teaching this class every Saturday morning helped him land an interview at Blue Mountain Retreat, he'd gladly instruct fifty people.

A swish of wind overhead set new green leaves in motion, and sunshine spilled through the branches to the ground. Michigan's Lake Endwell in mid-April brought hungry squirrels dashing across the soggy grass. Robins flitted here and there. The park throbbed with pent-up energy after a long winter. Bryan could relate.

His watch said 7:55. Had the Parks and Recreation Department listed the wrong date on the website or something?

One tiny woman with long brown hair clutched her hands together as she weaved across the pavement. She appeared to be praying or chanting or…something. *Odd.* Maybe she was taking one of those prayer walks or whatever it was Aunt Sally mentioned some of the church ladies started doing recently.

He stopped pacing. What if no one showed up?

People would come. They had to.

He couldn't spend the rest of his life surrounded by his happily married siblings, not when he would never have a wife and family of his own. He loved Lake Endwell, but his heart couldn't take it anymore. He needed the change Ontario, Canada, offered.

Blue Mountain Retreat was interviewing outdoor instructors in June. That left less than two months to strengthen his qualifications. The director wanted an experienced leader comfortable teaching an array of professional personalities from charismatic to timid to eccentric. The ideal candidate would have expert knowledge of North American forests and a diplomatic, outgoing personality.

Bryan had never been described as outgoing. His ex-wife had put it in less flattering terms. Boring. Lame. Hey, he might not be the most exciting person, but no local would refute his outdoor knowledge.

Now it was 7:58. Where was everyone?

He studied the parking lot again. A family unpacked bikes from a silver minivan. An elderly man hobbled in the direction of the bird feeders located near the pond. And the strange woman? Marched his way, albeit in a zigzag pattern.

As she neared, he pegged her at about five feet tall and in her late twenties, but he'd never been good at guessing ages. She had rosy lips and big green eyes that didn't seem to register her whereabouts. Streaks of cinnamon shot through her hair.

She was pretty.

Very pretty.

His pulse hammered like the bill of the downy wood-pecker against the poplar to his left. She could *not* be one of his students. He'd mentally prepared for older folks, college kids.

He hadn't prepared for pretty.

Green Eyes edged into the pavilion, her chest heaving as if she'd run six miles. Her face was white, and she blinked rapidly. "Is this the survival class?"

He widened his stance, crossing his arms over his chest. "Yes, this is Outdoor Survival 101."

"Good. I barely survived the parking lot, so I hope you know what you're doing."

Great. His only student. Cute and probably crazy.

Real funny, God. I ask You to get me out of my five-year rut, and You give me this?

"I know what I'm doing." Bryan rubbed the two-day stubble on his chin. "What was so bad about the parking lot?"

She grimaced, a visible shiver rippling over her. "Everything."

He pressed his lips together. He did not encourage overly dramatic behavior. His sister Libby's antics growing up had taught him that.

"Bryan Sheffield." He thrust his hand out. Her icy fingers felt fragile in his.

"Jade Emerson."

The name fit her on account of the eyes. "Since you're the lone student so far, let's wait a few minutes before heading to the trail."

Jade practically collapsed on the bench of a picnic table. Her olive jacket covered dark jeans, and she wore rubber rain boots—burgundy with black polka dots. She reminded him of a princess, someone he'd read about in picture books as a kid, but her defeated posture didn't match the images in his mind.

He hadn't seen her before, and in a small town like this it meant she wasn't from around here. One of his numerous relatives would have alerted him. Aunt Sally and the ladies from work were forever trying to set him up with any single woman in the county. He always politely declined, unwilling to reveal it wouldn't matter who they set him up with—he wasn't interested in dating or marriage. Once was enough.

"Are you from out of town?" he asked.

"Yes. Just moved yesterday."

He didn't know what it was like to be new in town. He'd lived here his entire life, but hopefully that would change this summer. "How did you find out about the class?"

She gave her head a little shake. "The website. I saw the class advertised a few weeks ago."

At least he knew the Parks and Recreation Department listed the correct information. "So where are you from?"

"Las Vegas." A bit of color returned to her cheeks.

"Sin City, huh?" Why would a pretty girl from Las Vegas want to move here?

"I prefer to think of it by its lesser known nickname, the Capital of Second Chances."

Second chances? A second chance at Blue Mountain sounded good. He hitched his chin. "So what brings you to Lake Endwell?"

"I'm opening a store." The words pulled from her as wispy and thin as threads of cotton candy.

"Oh, yeah? What kind?"

"A gift shop." She fanned herself, but the temperature couldn't be more than fifty-five degrees. "Custom-designed T-shirts and gifts. I'm still deciding on the inventory."

A candy store, novelty shop and higher-end women's clothing boutique satisfied the summer tourists. The town might not be able to support her store year-round, but Bryan kept his thoughts to himself. If Jade wanted to open a T-shirt shop, that was her business.

And his business? Wasn't looking promising, not with one student.

He checked the parking lot again. "It looks like you're the only one who showed up. Do you still want to take the class?"

"No."

No? His chest had a slow leak or something. He should be relieved. But her *no* stirred up bits and pieces he'd been suppressing all week, like the sinking feeling he got when his younger brother, Sam, sneered, *"You, teaching? You realize you'll have to leave the house and be friendly, right?"* As if Bryan had no social skills. He knew how to be friendly. But Sam's words had kicked up doubts. Would his personality kill his chances with the director of the retreat?

Jade stood on wobbly legs, and her fingertips darted to the table for support. "I don't want to take the class, but I will. I have to."

He pulled his shoulders back. A part of him would prefer no students to this one. Too cute. Too out there. Too everything. "I can cancel today's session."

"No!" Her eyes widened. "Don't do that."

"Why not?" He suppressed a sigh. Did she want to be here or not? Maybe this would qualify him for the eccentric personalities the retreat director mentioned.

She shook her head so rapidly her hair waved behind

her. Her face paled again. She wasn't going to faint, was she? Bryan stepped forward, but she remained standing.

"It will ruin everything."

Ruin what? He didn't know and wasn't asking. He'd grown up with two sisters. Their way of thinking had always been two steps ahead of his.

"Hey, it's okay. Don't get so worked up. We'll go to the trail right now. No big deal."

"The trail?" she squeaked. "Right now?"

"Yeah, isn't that what you want?"

"I… I…" Her hands twisted as if she were wringing out a wet washcloth. "I think I'm having a panic attack." Her breaths came in short, audible gasps.

"Here." He took a paper bag out of his backpack and handed it to her. "Breathe into this. When you've got it under control, tell me what's going on."

Jade slumped on the bench and sucked in a breath. The paper bag crinkled into itself. When she exhaled, it puffed out again. She didn't dare look at Bryan. First of all, he was a full foot taller than her, and her neck might snap trying to stare at him from her seated position. Secondly, the sight of him made her gooey insides extra mushy. His level of attractiveness on a scale of one to ten was a twenty. Those blue eyes reminded her of the desert sky, and he had a cleft in his chin. A cleft! No man should have such touchable dark blond hair.

And now he was restlessly waiting because he seemed to think she owed him an explanation. Which she did, after treating him to a full-blown episode of her ridiculous phobia. She pulled the bag away from her mouth.

"I don't like forests." *There.* She'd said it. And shoved the paper bag right back, daring him to mock her. His eyebrows drew together.

He probably couldn't comprehend the thought—him so tall, so fit, so at ease outdoors. He was practically perfect. She scowled. The guys she found attractive were always practically perfect—at first. Their charm wore off as they grew condescending, dismissive. *No, thanks.* She had enough on her hands getting her shop established.

"Why don't you like forests?"

A hysterical cackle rose in her throat, but she clamped her mouth shut, not allowing it to escape.

Why? Why indeed. Since her breathing had stabilized, she smoothed out the brown bag and set it on her lap. "I've never lived around many trees." Except for the summer in Germany when she was seven—her heartbeat grew faint as the memories returned. He didn't need to know her secrets. "They've always given me the creeps."

"Oh." He nodded, rubbing his chin.

Jade lightly massaged her temples. Trying to overcome this fear was impossible. It wasn't as if she hadn't tried numerous times. The excitement of quitting her job last month must have given her a false sense of power. Picking a town smack-dab in the middle of dense woods to open her business made no sense.

Except it did.

After Mimi died, Jade kept replaying the wisdom her grandmother shared over the years. One piece of advice had clung to her heart. *Jade, honey, I hope you find your Lake Endwell, a place where dreams come true. Poppi and I always said we'd move there, but God had other plans for us. Listen to His plan for your life.*

Moving here made perfect sense. Jade wanted her dreams—all of them—to come true.

"I'm missing something, right?" Bryan sounded uncertain. "If you don't like the forest, why did you move here?"

"It's complicated."

"Is there anything I can do?" He propped his foot on the bench.

She hoped so. She'd set her moving plans in motion after poking through Lake Endwell's website and stumbling across Bryan's class.

An answer to her prayer.

Living here wouldn't work unless she could tolerate trees. Yesterday she'd grown dizzy and hysterical driving through the tightly packed woods on the way into town. The thought of breaking down and getting lost… She shivered. How would she be able to make the thirty-minute drive to a mall, the discount stores or an airport unless she overcame this fear?

"I don't have any experience with not liking trees." Bryan's eyes clouded over. "Not sure I can be of much help."

Maybe Bryan's class was God's way of getting her here. Maybe He had another plan in mind for her to get over her affliction. Rising, she brushed off her jeans and willed her lips into a tight smile. "I'll figure something out." But what? She hadn't felt this torn since hearing Mimi had cancer.

"Well, the least I can do is show you around the park." His low, soothing voice unlatched the tightness around her chest. "You might not feel as scared if you know more about it."

She added *nice* to her mental list comprising Bryan Sheffield. But then, didn't they all seem nice at first? The nitpicking and disapproval began after they realized she wasn't as great as they'd first thought. The story of her dating life.

"You don't have to."

Bryan tilted his head. "You obviously want to get over

your fear or you wouldn't have shown up today. I'm no therapist, but I know my way around the woods."

"I must seem crazy." Jade wasn't a seven-year-old child anymore, and logically, she knew the chances of getting lost again were slim.

"Nah. I married crazy. You're…" Crimson climbed his neck. "Never mind. Follow me."

Married? Relief flooded her. Of course he was married. Married and safe. Now she wouldn't have to worry about being attracted to him. She'd promised herself no romance until she got the rest of her life in order and figured out the right type of guy for her.

"Grab the paper bag," Bryan said. "You might need it."

"Surviving in the woods depends on a lot of factors." Bryan kept his tone informal as they crossed a wide lawn toward a cluster of hardwoods. Why would anyone be afraid of trees? He could understand not wanting to hike for personal reasons, but to be afraid of the forest was a concept he couldn't wrap his head around.

Right after class, he was typing fliers. Posting them around town. Asking Aunt Sally and his sisters to spread the word far and wide. Advertising on the radio if need be. He'd have full attendance at next week's class. One student who was too scared to be out here would not qualify him for the job.

He needed that job.

Tuesday family dinners had become unbearable. All the private loving glances between Claire and Reed. The way Tommy glued himself to Stephanie's side. Jake and Libby's inside jokes. Bryan couldn't take it anymore. He just couldn't take the loneliness flooding him in their presence.

He glanced at Jade to make sure she wasn't hyperventilating again. She matched his pace. Quiet, but breathing normally.

Why had he encouraged her to stay? So her emotional state touched a nerve. It didn't mean she was his responsibility. He had no business spending time with someone so beautiful. And the slip about his marriage? Unraveled threads he'd fought to hide since Abby left. Yeah, she'd cheated on him, but he'd made vows, ones he didn't take lightly.

A part of him had known the marriage would never work. He'd ignored his instincts and asked her to marry him, anyway. He'd been dazzled by her style. Flattered by her pursuit of him. Fooled into believing she loved him as much as he loved her. No one to blame but himself.

Which was the bigger sin?

The divorce?

Or marrying her to begin with?

"Um, Bryan?" Jade tapped his arm. He almost jumped.

"Sorry," he said. "Yeah, so if you ever got lost in the woods…"

"Can we *not* mention getting lost?" Her serious tone made him smile.

"No problem." *Clear your head. It's been years since Abby left.* "Well, let's say you were hungry and didn't have anything to eat. There are plenty of edible plants if you know what to look for."

"I'll pack power bars and Tootsie Rolls."

"What if you got lost and ate your entire supply?"

"Didn't you get my memo about not discussing you-know-what?" She widened her eyes, her eyelashes curling upward.

"Right." He continued forward until stopping in front of a grouping of trees. Jade stood about ten feet away on the lawn. Once more Bryan was struck by her size.

A strong wind could blow her over as easily as a stray feather. He waved for her to approach. "Why don't you come here so I can show you what to look for?"

"I'm close enough."

He went back to her and waited. Why was she terrified? Was it because she was used to the desert? Had she been born afraid of forests? Or had she watched one too many horror films?

Finally, she sighed and followed him.

"This is a white birch." He got the impression she couldn't say a word and not from awe. He'd grown up hiking these woods with Granddad. Knew every bit of the surrounding area. He loved Lake Endwell—the evergreens, ferns, blue jays and sparrows, the scent of pollen, pinecones, the mucky ground after a hard rain. He loved it all. It would be tough to leave, but he couldn't stay.

Bryan peeled a six-inch section of birch bark and handed it to her. "It's textured on the outside but smooth inside. See? Smell it. It's a good smell."

The tight lines around her mouth eased. "It doesn't have much of a scent."

"Inhale. You'll catch it. Mint, with a bit of history."

"History?"

"Native Americans and early settlers relied on birch for a lot of things. It's waterproof, so they used it for roofs, canoes, even shoes. The inner bark is edible."

"I didn't know that. It peels off in ribbons." She inspected the strip, picking at the pale pink layers. He took it as a good sign.

"You can write on it, too. Take it home. Try it."

"Okay."

Bryan tugged a slim branch to her. She hopped with her hand over her heart. He moved it back several inches. The suppleness of new tree growth always impressed him because of the resilience. Age strengthened the wood. "Sycamore trees have white bark also, but it's not papery like the birch's. If you aren't sure if a tree is a sycamore or a birch, check the leaves. Birch trees have small, oval-shaped leaves. Sycamore leaves are big and shaped like a hand." He held his palm up, fingers together, to show her.

Jade rose on her tiptoes and extended her neck. "Why does it matter if I know which is which?"

"Survival." Bryan let the branch spring back into place. "The white birch has pure, drinkable sap. It's sweet. If you had a Swiss Army knife on you, you'd have a potential source of hydration. Chop a small triangle out of the trunk, and you can catch the moisture and eat the inner flesh."

"Couldn't I drink from that?" Rotating to the side, she pointed to the pond.

"You could, but you'd have to boil the water first. It's full of algae and other contaminants. Besides, you might be somewhere where there isn't a water source." He spotted an overgrowth of weeds. "Before we continue, I have to warn you about certain plants."

"Great," she muttered, but joined him.

"Over there." He nodded to a green vine. "That's poison ivy. You can tell because it has three pointy green leaves."

Jade hung back, flourishing her hand in the direction of the weeds. "Is that poison ivy, too?"

"No. That's honeysuckle. It has individual leaves." He didn't dare lop off the poison ivy, but she didn't seem to be willing to come near it. "I'm not sure if you can see this, but all three leaves are coming from the same stem."

"Oh. Okay, I get it."

Bryan returned to her side. "Poison oak has three

leaves also. There's a saying in the woods, 'Leaves of three, let it be.' Avoid them or you might get a rash."

"Avoiding them won't be a problem." She lifted one shoulder and smiled. Once more, he was all too aware of her appeal. She was even prettier when she wasn't terrified. She tapped her finger against her chin. "You know, I don't feel as nervous right now."

"Good. Now that you live in Lake Endwell, you might find hiking becomes your new hobby. Nature is generous. Give it a chance."

"Hiking as my hobby? Doubtful." Jade tucked the birch bark into her jacket pocket. "What do you mean, nature is generous?"

He plucked a young blade of grass from the ground and held it out. "It's all connected. The ground gives nutrients to the plants, and the plants provide food and shelter for the birds, insects and animals. Everything you see in this park is generous."

"I never thought of it that way." Shielding her eyes, she raised her face to the sky. "I'm not sure I'm ready for all this."

"Take it one day at a time."

"But that's the thing. I'm kind of okay now, but I know we're not going to stand on the lawn for two hours next week."

"No," he murmured. He hadn't considered she'd want to continue taking his class, not when she could barely tolerate the birches. "We won't."

"I think I've had enough forest-related instruction for the day." A breeze lifted the ends of her hair. "Can we check out the pond?"

"Sure."

Side by side they squished through the grass.

"Do you come here a lot with your wife?"

Bryan almost stumbled. He had that one coming. He shouldn't have said anything. Shouldn't have mentioned a wife.

He might be divorced, but it didn't mean he was single.

"No," he said. "I can't say I do."

Chapter Two

Why hadn't he told Jade the truth?

Bryan tossed his keys on the foyer's rickety table in the tan bungalow he shared with Sam. Days like this he missed coming home to his older brother, Tommy. For years the two of them lived here, watching baseball, ordering pizzas and sharing the silent bond of failed marriages. But Tommy was happily married again, living two miles away in a new house near the lake with his daughter and pregnant wife.

Continuing into the kitchen, Bryan opened the fridge and grabbed a bottle of iced tea. The fact Tommy had created a future for himself made Bryan want to believe it was possible for him, too.

However, Tommy had remarried his ex-wife. Bryan would never remarry Abby. For one thing, she'd gotten hitched two weeks after their divorce was final. For another, she didn't love him. Probably never had. Their marriage had lacked substance. Didn't make their split any less painful, though.

He padded across the worn carpeting and dropped onto the beat-up leather couch.

"Anybody home?" Dad called from the front door.

After wiping his work boots on the mat, he tugged them off and took a seat in the recliner next to the couch. "How did your class go?"

"Okay." Bryan drummed his fingers on the arm of the couch.

"Lots of folks show up?"

"Only one."

Dad raised his eyebrows. "One, huh?"

"Yeah, and she probably won't be back. I'm typing up fliers later. I'll get more people next week."

"This class is important to you, isn't it?"

A twinge of guilt poked at his conscience. Bryan had always been close to his father. Dad had done a good job raising the five of them after Mom died. But Dale Sheffield could *not* keep a secret, and the last thing Bryan wanted was town gossips whispering about his plans. They'd chattered for months about Abby's indiscretions and the subsequent divorce. He'd just as soon drive pine needles under his fingernails than have the citizens of Lake Endwell discussing his life ever again.

Sam appeared from the hallway leading to the bedrooms. He yawned, shoving his hand through rumpled hair. "Hey, Dad. Bryan."

"You look like you need a pot of coffee," Dad said. "Or are you sick?"

"Long night. I'm hiring an assistant manager. The new dealership took off better than I expected." Sam plopped onto the couch next to Bryan. His black basketball shorts and faded green tee made him look more like a college student than the CEO of Sheffield Auto. Sam had opened his own dealership after Christmas, which brought the total to five across three counties. Bryan managed two and Tommy the other two. "How did your class go?"

"Only one girl showed up," Dad said. "She might not be back."

Sam snorted, grinning. "Way to go, Bry. You scared her off, didn't you?"

Bryan squirmed. He hadn't scared her off. Not in the way Sam implied.

But you lied to her.

"Don't say that." Dad frowned. "Bryan knows the woods better than anyone, except maybe your grand-dad, may he rest in peace."

"Yeah, yeah." Sam reached for the remote and cocked an eyebrow at Bryan. "I still don't know why you put the course together. This whole thing is pretty random, if you ask me."

Bryan didn't answer. His little brother noticed too much.

"Bryan is sharing his knowledge," Dad said. "My father would want him to. I don't remember you ever wanting to get your feet muddy in the woods. Maybe you should take the class."

What a horrible idea. Bryan glowered at the bottle of iced tea in his hand. He didn't need Sam making wise-cracks while he tried to teach. It was difficult enough getting the students there. He didn't want to fight for their respect, too.

"I'm more brains than brawn." Sam tapped his temple.

Bryan sniffed. "More mouth than anything."

"Hey, my conversation skills made up for your si-lence. You barely said a word to Lily and Kayla last weekend."

Dad cocked his head to the side. "Who are Lily and Kayla?"

Sam stretched his arms over his head and yawned

again. "Paulette insisted we meet her cousin's daughter and friend."

"Roxanne and Paulette are as bad as Aunt Sally." Bryan screwed the cap back on the iced tea and set the bottle on the end table.

"Worse," Sam said. "Kayla and Lily were nice and all, but I don't need to be set up, especially not by middle-aged meddlers at work. I can find a date on my own." He jerked his thumb at Bryan. "Now, this one needs all the help he can get."

"Leave me out of it." Bryan lurched to his feet. "I don't want help."

"Sure you don't. You're a real dating machine."

"That's it." Dad rose, holding his hands out. "I'm tired of you two arguing. I've been saying it for months—this living arrangement isn't working out. Maybe it's time for one of you to move."

"No…" Bryan shut his mouth. He'd almost blurted Sam would have the place to himself if Bryan moved to Canada this summer. If he didn't keep a tighter lid on his plans, the whole family would be lining up to talk him out of them. He already dreaded their inevitable rant about his commitment to Sheffield Auto if he got the job. "We're fine, Dad. Just messing with each other."

"Don't take things too far." Dad gave them both a long look before asking Sam who he had in mind for the assistant manager position. Bryan let out a breath.

One problem averted. What about the other?

In this tiny town, Jade would find out soon enough he wasn't married. He should have told her the truth right away. He didn't want her first impression of him to be a lie. It took a lot of courage for her to come today.

It wouldn't be hard to find her. He'd call Aunt Sally.

He owed Jade the truth.

* * *

This place was quiet. Too quiet. Dusk had fallen, which meant Jade would be exposed to outside eyes as soon as she turned the lights on.

Buy curtains.

Another thing to add to her list. Not tonight, though.

Jade sank low into her navy couch. People said small towns were so cozy and great to live in, but this silence felt eerie. Where were the traffic sounds, planes flying overhead and sirens? Without having her cable hooked up, she couldn't turn on her television for companion noise. What she did hear unnerved her. The wind made a rippling whoosh through the siding every now and then, and the relentless *drip, drip* of the bathroom sink matched the pulse pounding in her temples.

Would she ever be comfortable enough to call this town home?

She yawned, not bothering to cover her mouth. At least she'd made a dent in the unpacking. After her embarrassing hyperventilation session with Bryan, she'd driven back to the one-bedroom apartment above her soon-to-be store. A set of stairs outside led to the tiny kitchen with cabinets painted gray. Newer dark laminate countertops were speckled with silver flecks. In the front of the apartment was a decent-size living room complete with beige walls and tan carpet. A short hall revealed a bathroom and her bedroom—beige, of course.

She loved every square inch of it.

A knocking sound came from the kitchen. Jade shot to her feet, grabbed the empty bronze candleholder from the end table and crept through the piles of boxes in the kitchen. Another knock sounded.

Just the door. She exhaled, setting the candleholder on the counter, and opened the door a sliver.

"Hi." Bryan loomed in the doorway. He appeared taller and his shoulders broader than when they were outside earlier. "Sorry to bother you, but I, well, I need to talk to you about something."

Her heartbeat galloped, partly because he was even more handsome than she remembered, and also because he'd tracked her down like some sort of stalker. Had he followed her here? She remained behind the door, using it as a shield. "How did you know where I lived?"

"My aunt Sally. Sorry, I'm not a creeper. I didn't follow you or anything. It's just, well, nothing is a secret in this town. Aunt Sally is friends with Jules Reichert."

"My landlord."

"Yep."

What did he want to talk to her about? He probably felt sorry for her. Or was asking her not to come to class because she needed professional guidance. So help her, if he handed her the card of a therapist to work through her fears, she'd rip it up in front of him. She'd tried counseling. It hadn't worked. She would only try it again if truly desperate.

"I didn't mean to interrupt you, but I need to clear something up. You could call it a confession." Bryan shifted from one foot to the other.

A confession? Her spirits perked right up. Confessions didn't involve condescending advice about her problem.

"Yeah, so earlier, I made it sound as if I'm married, but I got divorced almost five years ago."

"Oh." Divorced. There went his unavailable status, which was too bad, because him being single complicated things. The fact he'd found her to clear up a tiny misunderstanding said a lot about his character, though.

"Um, I—" he massaged the back of his neck "—well, it was wrong of me to mislead you."

She prepared to give him her thanks-for-stopping-by speech, but he looked so contrite and uncomfortable on her doorstep. Sympathy overrode her good judgment.

"It's not a big deal." She leaned against the doorframe. She'd play it cool. Pretend she wasn't attracted to him in the slightest. "I just want to be able to live here and drive to Target or a shopping mall, and, you know, go to one of the parks without hyperventilating."

His lips lifted into a lopsided grin. "I could help with that."

"I don't know if anyone can help. I'm not exactly the ideal student."

"Yeah, but you're my only student. I can't afford to be picky." His blue eyes teased, and her tummy flipped.

"That's true." She nodded in mock sincerity. Why couldn't she say goodbye and close the door? Flirting with him would get her heart in trouble the way flirting always did. When would she learn? Still, she didn't know anyone here, and loneliness weighed heavily on her shoulders.

"Have you eaten yet?" he asked. "There's a pizza place around the corner."

Her stomach rumbled. Empty, silent apartment? Or pizza with all-wrong-for-her Bryan Sheffield? Before she could talk herself out of it, she nodded. "Let me grab my purse, and I'll meet you outside."

Less than a minute later, she joined him on the sidewalk in front of her building. No light poured from the large front window, making the store appear abandoned. The chilly air slipped under her collar. She zipped her jacket to her neck.

"This way," Bryan said.

Jade fell in beside him. The sun had gone to sleep, and the stars blinked on one by one in the clear, ink-black sky.

"I can't remember the last time I stepped out at night and saw such bright stars."

"Really?" He kept his hands in his pockets.

"Yeah, I grew up in a seventies ranch house in Winchester, a suburb of Las Vegas not too far from downtown. City lights hazed the sky." A far cry from her current rural address.

"I've never spent much time in the city."

"No? The air smells different here." Jade tried to pinpoint the source. If she had to label it, she'd call it fresh.

"What does it smell like in Vegas?" His unhurried strides made it easy for her to keep pace with him.

"It depends. If you're on the sidewalks of the Strip, you'll smell gasoline fumes, exhaust from the line of taxis and cigarette smoke. Basically, you'll smell cigarettes everywhere outside in Las Vegas."

"Can't say I'm a fan of those."

"Me, neither. I worked for an advertising company geared to the hotels. I loathed crossing through the lobbies when I had to go on-site and not just because they reeked of cologne. The colors, noises and smells were an assault on the senses."

"Advertising, huh?"

"Yep." She rubbed her cold hands together. "The competitive job atmosphere wasn't my thing. Too cutthroat." She'd never had the heart to play politics the way her coworkers had. If they wanted an account, they did whatever it took to land it, even if it meant taking credit for someone else's work or schmoozing people they didn't care for.

"Did you like living in Vegas?"

Mimi's smiling face came to mind. So many good memories. "Yes. It was home. Living in Michigan is going to be an adjustment." She burrowed deeper into her jacket. "The main reason I loved it there was because of my grandmother. I lived with her most of my life. Poppi worked at Nellis Air Force Base, and after he died, Mimi didn't want to move."

"So you lived with your grandmother until now?" He didn't sound judgmental, merely curious.

"Well, there were a few months on my own in New York City, but Mimi got stomach cancer, and I moved back in with her."

"To take care of her."

"Yeah. She raised me." Those terrible final weeks with Mimi had been excruciating, yet in many ways, joyful, too. Hospice had helped Mimi die peacefully. Jade had no doubt she and Mimi would be having cozy conversations in heaven for eternity. "I hope you don't think I did it out of duty. I loved her."

"She passed, then?" When they reached Main Street, he turned left.

"Two months ago."

Jade paused as Bryan opened the wooden door of a brick storefront. Light spilled onto the sidewalk from the huge window. Lake Endwell Pizza was etched in bold black letters with a traditional font. Not flashy, but good, smart branding. A little round table for two had been centered under the window, and a young couple simultaneously reached for slices, then laughed as cheese stretched from their pizza back to the metal pan.

"You coming?" He swept his hand for her to enter. She savored the aroma of oregano and garlic and enjoyed the warmth of the room. He led her to a rectangular table for four next to an exposed brick wall. Teenagers clad in black tees, jeans and white aprons joked behind the counter. Most of the tables, all wooden, were occupied.

No one looked out of place here. Jeans, sweaters and hoodies ruled.

Bryan scrutinized a menu as if it held the secret to world peace. She didn't bother picking one up. Three women in their fifties laughed at something, and Jade smiled. Their happiness was contagious.

"What toppings do you like?" He peered over the menu.

"Anything but onions. Oh, and no anchovies."

His lips curved up, and her breath caught in her throat. *What a smile.* Maybe she would have been better off staying home in her empty apartment. She had a bad habit of falling for a killer smile, then being left to pick up the pieces when its owner vanished.

A scrawny teen with a pen in one hand and a slim pad of paper in the other appeared next to their table. "What can I get you?"

They ordered drinks and the Deluxe minus onions, and the kid disappeared.

She tilted her head to the side. "So is this the best pizza place in town or the only one?"

"The best."

"Hey, Bryan." A tall, dark-haired man waved and approached their table. Following him was a stunning young woman with long blond hair, dark skinny jeans and a baby-blue sweater that perfectly matched her cornflower eyes. They made a striking couple. The blondie kept tugging on the man's arm, shaking her head and whispering something.

The muscle in Bryan's cheek flickered. "Libby. Jake."

Jade's brain went into overdrive. Who was this mystery couple whom Bryan clearly didn't want to see?

"Jade—" his eyes were all apology "—this is my little sister, Libby, and her husband, Jake."

"Hi, nice to meet you." Jade shifted and smiled.

"My pleasure." Libby backed up a step. "We won't keep you."

"You don't mind, do you?" Jake pulled out the chair next to Bryan and sat.

"We don't want to interrupt." Libby gave Jake a pointed glare.

"But, Libby, all the tables are full." Jake grabbed a menu. "I'm starving."

"Please, join us." Jade gestured to the empty chair next to hers. Libby draped her purse over the back of it.

Bryan asked Jake about his job, but his eyes met Jade's. Questions lurked in there, ones she couldn't decipher.

"So, Jade, tell me all about yourself." Libby gave Jade her full attention. She beamed with interest…and hope. Why the hope?

"What do you want to know?"

"How did you meet my brother?"

"Well, I moved here yesterday…"

"Oh! The T-shirt shop, right? You're in Mrs. Reichert's building around the corner. I think it's a fantastic idea."

Jade didn't know how to respond. How did Libby know so much?

Bryan's eyes glimmered with amusement as he said, "No secrets in this town."

Apparently not. "Yes, I specialize in custom-designed shirts."

"Embroidered?" Libby splayed hot-pink fingernails on the table. Jade couldn't help but be charmed.

"Sometimes. Mostly I make standard screen prints, but I enjoy playing around with glitter lettering, rhinestones and shimmer decals."

"Glitter and sparkles?" Jake snorted. "Sounds right up Libby's alley."

Libby's laugh tinkled. "Exactly. You'll have to show me some of your designs."

"I'd love to."

"So how did you two meet?" Libby's lips parted slightly as she gestured to Bryan, then to Jade.

"Jade's from Las Vegas. She's taking my outdoor course." The way Bryan said it discouraged additional questions. A point in Bryan's favor. He was discreet.

"Outdoor class." Libby made a face and stuck her tongue out. "Don't tell me you're a nature nut, too, Jade."

"No." She grinned. "I can't say I am."

"That's a relief." Libby brought her hand to her lips. "Oh, me and my big mouth. What if you were obsessed with the outdoors? My sister, Claire, is always saying I need to think before I speak."

Jade laughed. "I wouldn't be offended. I don't know much about nature."

"Well, Bryan will help you. He knows everything there is to know about trees, bugs, fishing, making a fire. He'll go on for hours about soil and worms and how the silver undersides of leaves mean rain's coming." Libby turned her attention to Bryan. "I mean that in the nicest possible way."

His jaw clenched, but he didn't reply.

Libby continued. "Talk about uncanny. I mean, you moved here yesterday, you want to learn about nature *and* Bryan just happened to be teaching a class this morning. It's as if God planned it."

Jade did a double take. She'd thought the same, but hearing it from a stranger? She stole a peek at Bryan. He frowned as though he, too, pondered Libby's words.

"What's Las Vegas like?" Jake asked. "I've never been there."

All the things Jade loved about it bubbled up inside.

"It's hot, loud and over-the-top. A fun place to visit. There's so much to do—that is, if you can handle the crowds."

"I'm not much of a crowd person." Jake grinned.

"Tell me about it." Libby shook her head. "That leaves you out, too, Bryan."

Everything Libby was saying didn't add up to the picture Jade had been painting of Bryan, the one where he was another too-good-to-be-true guy poised to let her down.

It didn't matter. Jade was *not* interested.

"How many are in your family?" Jade asked Libby.

"Depends on how you define family," Libby said. "There are five of us kids. Add Jake, Reed, Stephanie and Macy, plus Dad. And Aunt Sally and Uncle Joe, and…"

Libby listed more names, but the pizza arrived. Bryan dished out the slices. Half an hour later, Jake and Bryan paid the bill, and they all walked Jade back to her apartment.

"It's so cute." Libby stopped in front of the store. "If you need help with decorating or anything, call me."

"Thanks." Jade liked Libby already. "Do you all want to come up? It's a disaster, but…"

"Oh, no," Libby said. "We'll let you settle in. It was nice to meet you."

With his arm slung over her shoulders, Jake steered Libby in the opposite direction.

The air had grown even cooler, and Jade shivered under her coat.

"So," she said. "I guess I'll see you next week."

He frowned. "You still want to come to the classes?"

"Yeah, why?" Had he changed his mind during pizza or something? If he told her he wouldn't teach her anymore, she didn't know what she'd do. Her backup plan was dicey and not well thought out. Sure, she could try finding another counselor, but would that cure her when past sessions had failed? She was counting on Bryan's class. Lake Endwell was too important—the key to her dream life. She didn't want to start over somewhere else.

"More people will be there," he said. "You might not be ready to go into the woods."

"Oh, right." Her good mood disappeared. She'd assumed she'd be the only one to show up, the way she'd been today. But he was correct. If more people came, she wouldn't be ready to hike in the woods. It might take weeks—months—for her to be prepared. An overwhelming urge to crawl into bed and duck under the covers came over her.

"What are you doing tomorrow afternoon?" The intensity in his stare made her blink twice, and her pulse quickened.

"Unpacking, why?"

"Maybe I can get you up to speed so you can continue the classes."

He clearly didn't know what he was up against.

A Bavarian cottage at the foot of the famed Black Forest. The last week of her summer in Germany. Those mean neighbor boys playing a trick on her.

Why had she been so trusting?

She tucked her hair behind her ear. "You don't have to…"

"Yeah, I do. Libby was right. The timing and everything."

"Honestly, you don't…"

Bryan took a step closer. Her nerves twitched like Mexican jumping beans.

"Meet me at Evergreen Park around two o'clock." He gently took her by the elbow. "I'll walk you up."

Jade climbed the steps to her apartment with Bryan directly behind her. Once she unlocked the door, she opened it and faced him. "Thanks for the pizza."

He nodded. "Will I see you tomorrow?"

"I'll think about it."

"I'll be there, whatever you decide."

She slipped inside and locked the door behind her.

She'd lived here all of twenty-four hours and already teetered on the edge of the danger zone. Not that Bryan seemed interested, but still. She couldn't help being attracted to him.

Hadn't she promised herself to keep her priorities straight? First on the list was opening the store. Second was overcoming her fear of the woods. She had no business beyond friendship with anyone until she figured out what she'd been doing wrong in her previous relationships.

After tossing her purse on the table, she padded down the hall to her bedroom. Maybe she was overtired. She barely knew Bryan.

Libby was right. God planned the outdoor class. He was helping free her from the chains paralyzing her. Maybe Bryan had the key to unlock them.

God, what do I do? Go to the park tomorrow? Even though I think he's really cute and seems nice and honest? Or is this a test? Are You checking to see if I was serious about not dating?

Jade fell back onto the bed and stared at the ceiling. She'd sleep on it.

"I assume the move was successful." Jade's mother had a distinct accent. Part American, part French with a hint of German. Her rich alto voice matched her vast intelligence. "Did you hire the moving company I recommended?"

Jade had been unpacking all morning, trying to decide if meeting Bryan at the park would be smart or dumb. She propped her cell phone between her ear and shoulder. "Hello to you, too, Mom. I rented a U-Haul. I'm proud to say, I drove it here all by myself."

Her mother didn't answer. Jade surveyed the boxes piled high that still needed to be dealt with. Her dining table overflowed with odds and ends. Where was she supposed to put everything?

"You know how I feel about U-Hauls," Mom finally said. "I don't understand why you didn't hire the company I emailed you about."

The company had given Jade an estimate of over five thousand dollars, that was why.

"They were pricey, Mom."

"I told you I would pay for it."

"No, thanks." She poked through a box and pulled out an adorable silver lamp with a paisley navy and cream shade she bought from a thrift shop. "I'm twenty-seven years old."

"What does your age have to do with your safety? Tell me you didn't hire a stranger to unload the truck when you got to town. He could have murdered you."

"Actually, I did hire a stranger. I googled 'moving companies who hire serial killers' and requested the freakiest-looking guy they had."

White noise didn't cover the icy stillness. "That's not funny, Jade Marie."

"Just my twisted attempt at a joke." She added *Stop baiting Mom* to her mental to-do list.

"I don't approve of you taking unnecessary chances, and I'm not pleased you moved to the middle of nowhere."

When had Mom ever approved of her decisions? "Don't worry, when I arrived in Lake Endwell, I hired a reputable service to unload the truck. Yes, I checked their references. They did a good job. Anyway, how is Gerald? Have you two found a breakthrough on the cancer trial yet?"

"He's fine, and negative on the breakthrough, but we're working on a fascinating hypothesis..." Excitement colored her mother's words. Jade's stepfather, Gerald, and her mother worked in Lyons, France, for the World Health Organization. Both renowned cancer researchers, the two were perfect for each other. Jade's father, on the other hand, was a celebrated heart surgeon at the Mayo Clinic in Phoenix, Arizona, where he lived with his second wife, a board member of a nonprofit for underprivileged children.

Brilliant. All of them.

And generous.

Good people.

Sometimes Jade felt bad her exceptional parents had produced such an ordinary child. She'd brought home Bs and Cs on her report cards. Flunked math in third grade. Didn't make varsity tennis. Didn't win a single match. She'd chosen a nonmedical field of study. She hadn't even graduated with honors. It was a wonder her mother still talked to her. Her father certainly didn't.

"...the cells stopped replicating... Jade, are you listening?"

"Yes, Mom." Jade wadded a piece of packing paper and looked for a wastebasket. She opened the cupboard under the sink. Did she own trash bags? Nope. She tossed the paper on the floor. "I hope the replicating thingy gets the results you want."

"Not a 'thingy.' It's... Never mind. The world is relying on us. Now, listen, this move of yours might not work out, and I think you should consider an alternate plan. We'll get you settled in an apartment in Paris. Gerald's sister's friend works at a prestigious advertising company. It would mean working at an entry-level position in marketing, but you'd have a job. Just don't…"

Jade held her breath. *Don't say it, Mom.*

"Just don't settle."

Her shoulders drooped. She'd heard it a million times. At first, she thought it meant something good, that she was special and deserved more, but as she matured, Jade realized her mom actually meant, *Don't disappoint me.*

Her mother sighed. "This T-shirt thing was acceptable while you were in college, but you need to think of your future. And the world's future. We're all in this together, you know. How will T-shirts help society? Think about it."

"Okay, Mom. I will." Society always ranked high on her mother's list of priorities. "Listen, I'm practically wading in boxes. Can I let you go? I'll never get them unpacked if I don't."

"Certainly."

"Give my best to Gerald."

"Will do. *Au revoir.*"

Jade pressed End on her phone and set it on the counter. She didn't want to save the world. She just wanted to design some shirts. Was that so wrong?

Mom meant well. Truly, she did. And she had a point about helping society. Did the world need another gift shop? Probably not. But designing T-shirts all through college had been fun. More fulfilling than advertising. An entry-level job in marketing sounded awful, even if it was in Paris. And Mom and Gerald lived five hours away. Five hours or fifteen hours wouldn't make a difference. Jade would be on her own in Paris or Lake Endwell.

Alone and lonely.

The past two months without Mimi clawed at Jade's chest. She grabbed a framed photo of them off the floor and carried it into the living room. Using her sleeve, she swiped the dust off an end table, placing the picture on top.

Mimi, you would tell me to go to the park today. You'd encourage me to open the store. You'd tell me I'm brave. I won't let you down.

She glanced at the clock. She had just enough time to meet Bryan.

Chapter Three

"You made it." Bryan waited for Jade as she approached the pavilion. Part of him had hoped she wouldn't show up today. But the other part, the irrational side, had been searching the parking lot for her cherry-red compact car.

"I made it." Jade's pale face and jerky movements said it all.

If the forest was too much for her, Bryan could at least say he tried to help. He'd move forward with his class guilt-free. And if she did make it into the woods? She'd be one more student to add to his spreadsheet along with the hours and skills he taught each week. He'd typed and printed fliers after church this morning, and Dad and Aunt Sally promised to help distribute them to local businesses tomorrow. Next Saturday would be different. He'd have a full class. With or without Jade.

"I did some research about overcoming fears." Bryan gestured for her to join him. She trembled beneath her puffy black vest. She'd pulled her hair back in some sort of braid. Black jeans and a pair of lace-up hiking boots completed her outfit. She looked cute. And terrified. "Have you heard of exposure therapy?"

"Yes. I've heard of it. One therapist wanted me to try flooding."

"Then you've been through therapy? I read about flooding. Total immersion, right? That's kind of extreme." He pushed up the sleeves of his fleece pullover. The websites he'd skimmed last night had given him ideas how to help her, but he didn't want to push her or accidentally make things worse. He wasn't used to offering advice unless it had to do with an automobile. "I figured you were basically trying the exposure method by coming to my class, so you might try some gradual things I read about on a few websites."

She wrapped her arms around herself. "Sure. I've read them, too. Step one, look at pictures of trees. Step two, watch a video of the forest. Step three, come to Evergreen Park."

"See," he said, smiling. "You're already a quarter-way through the list."

"Remind me again, what's step four?"

"Honestly, I don't know. I didn't memorize them, and I forgot the printout at home. But if you want, we'll go to the blue path."

She blinked rapidly, and he heard her breathing quicken.

He straightened his arms, palms out. "We're not walking *on* the path. Just standing at the entrance."

Her fingertips fluttered to her throat. "Okay."

They strolled along the grass. The weather was still cool, and the air hinted at rain later.

"Sorry my sister barged into dinner last night. My family can come on kind of strong."

"I like Libby," she said softly. "She's welcoming. And Jake seems nice."

"Yeah, he is. He's good for Libby. Keeps her grounded. She's good for him, too." Bryan glanced at her. "Are you doing okay?"

"So far." She moved stiffly. "How many times have you taught Outdoor Survival 101?"

"None. This is my first time."

"Really? You're good at it. You're patient. And knowledgeable."

The compliment filled him, made him stand taller. Helping Jade might be beneficial to both of them. His conversation skills could use a boost. Talking about facts and figures was easy. Random chatter was beyond him.

"Tell me more about your store," he said. "It looked empty last night."

"It is empty. I ordered a printing machine and an engraver. I'm still researching what furniture I want to use to display everything. The rooms need a coat of paint, too. I'm excited to get started."

"How did you get into T-shirt designing?" Bryan enjoyed the way her face brightened when she discussed the store.

"I got a part-time job at a novelty shop right after I graduated from high school. I loved working there. My boss taught me everything—all the secrets to making quality designs. It's the only thing I'm truly good at."

"I know the feeling. I'm good at running my car dealerships, but this—" he stretched his arm out "—I'm best outdoors."

"I can tell." She smiled up at him, and he gulped. He'd known he was lighting matches over dry tinder when he'd invited her today. Her easy manner and open smile made him want to offer things he shouldn't. Last night, Libby's crack about God's plan had hit a nerve. The more he'd thought about it, the more he was convinced helping Jade *was* God's plan. At least for today.

He pressed forward. "Almost there."

* * *

"I don't like this." Jade studied the path entrance, then closed her eyes. Impressions from twenty years ago flooded her. Clutching Charlie, her stuffed puppy. Being surrounded by trees, trying to keep up with the boys, but they ran too fast, their laughter fading. Branches and leaves had scratched at her cheeks, her hair, her clothes. Which way to turn? Where was the path?

She opened her eyes again. A wide paved lane stood before her, and a light gust of wind lifted the end of her braid.

This fear was too big. She needed more than an outdoor guide. She needed shock therapy or something.

Attitude, Jade.

Mimi would say nothing was too big for God. Until Jade turned twelve, she'd prayed every night for the Lord to cure her, but the panic remained, so she figured God's answer was *no*, and she'd stopped praying about it.

"Let's stay here a minute." Bryan's tall, athletic presence reassured her.

"We skipped about five steps on the therapy list."

"You're doing good." His fleece-covered arm brushed her sleeve.

She physically restrained herself from clinging to him and begging him to take her away from this place. Why couldn't she be normal? All the pep talks she'd given herself over the past weeks had been pointless. Anxiety ruled her outdoor life.

He touched her hand. "Jade?"

"Oh! What? Sorry, didn't hear you."

"I didn't say anything."

"Oh, you didn't." She shook her spinning head. The ground wasn't as firm beneath her new boots as it had been near the pavilion. The opening of the path was close. Too close. Nausea threatened.

"Maybe this is a mistake," Bryan said. "You don't look so great."

She willed her lungs to accept more air than the shallow breaths they currently allowed. "Gee, thanks."

"That's not what I meant." He looked up at the sky.

She didn't need to gaze upward to see a drop cloth of gray. If the sun would come out, maybe the scene in front of her wouldn't appear as sinister. Actually, the view didn't match the one in her mind. The blue path cut through scattered trees, not a thick forest like in Germany, and mallards quacked overhead. Happy sounds.

"My grandfather took me here all the time when I was younger. I know every inch of these woods. You'll never get lost with me by your side."

She didn't doubt him. He exuded confidence out here. Maybe if she tethered herself to him, she could take a few steps in there without breaking out in a terrified sweat.

"I miss Granddad." Bryan crouched and picked up an acorn. "Wish I could hike with him one more time."

"I understand." She fought the urge to close her eyes again. "I wish I could have coffee with Mimi again. Sounds as if you and your grandfather were close."

"We were. Mom died when I was eight. Granddad and I spent a lot of time together after her death. Dad had his hands full with the babies—Sam and Libby. My other sister, Claire, was still little, but I'm pretty sure she considered the young ones hers, so she helped Dad. My older brother, Tommy, came with Granddad and me to hike and fish, but after a couple of years it was just the two of us."

"Why didn't Tommy go anymore?"

Bryan grinned. "He discovered sports."

"You're not into sports?"

"I played some, but I liked being outside with Grand-dad better."

She relaxed a fraction and squinted, attempting to see the trees in a different light.

"I hope you don't mind me asking, but did something happen to frighten you?"

"You could say that." She shoved her hands in the pockets of her vest. "It was a long time ago."

He edged closer. His tall, solid frame comforted her for some reason. Made her want to lean in, rely on him to protect her out here.

Not smart. He'd leave her. Everyone else did.

"How long ago?" Bryan flicked the acorn into a bush.

"Oh, I was little." Did she want to talk about this? Mimi had tried to help, but every time they neared a wooded area, Jade had grown hysterical. Eventually Mimi stopped trying and told her there were some things best left to God.

"How little?" Bryan asked. "Toddler or teenager?"

"In between. I was seven." A nervous laugh escaped, and her shoulders tensed until they reached her ears. All alone in Germany. Mom was at work. The neighbor boys had gotten a kick out of playing a prank on her, leaving her alone, wandering. Sweat broke out on her forehead. "It's not something I talk about."

Understanding flashed in his eyes. "Fair enough." He motioned for her to follow him to a park bench several feet away.

Jade perched on it, facing what looked like a Christmas tree. She loved Christmas. Not all trees were bad.

Bryan leaned forward, resting his elbows on his knees. "I had nightmares after my mom died."

She knew all about nightmares, too. "Yeah, I have bad dreams—well, one bad dream. About the forest."

"Is it night or day?"

"Night."

"Would it be as bad if it were daytime?" he asked.

"I think so."

"Why?"

"It's so dark, it doesn't matter if it's night or day. I'm alone. There's no path. Everything closes in, the leaves and branches grab me."

His serious expression assured her he didn't think she was silly, or if he did, he was good at hiding it.

"What are you trying to do in the dream?"

"Escape. I want out of there."

"But there's no way out."

"Exactly."

"Do you run?"

"Eventually." The branches always tore at her face and hands, and she'd fall to her knees, sobbing in terror as orange and yellow eyes multiplied. She didn't want to talk about it anymore. "Tell me what's so great about this place."

Bryan took the change in subject in stride. "Spring brings Lake Endwell back to life. Next week you'll see wildflowers popping up. Squirrels say hello when you wind through the path. Inhale and you smell it all—the earth, air, pollen—and it's good."

"I think I'd rather light a candle in the safety of my home."

"Give it a chance. Beats any candle. The weather will warm up soon, and you'll really have fun. Swimming, fishing, bonfires. This area is all about the outdoors." He brushed something from her shoulder. She hoped it wasn't a bug. "What did you feel when we stood in front of the path?"

What did she feel?

Overwhelmed, claustrophobic. Scared.

Several birds flew past, and in the distance she heard birds calling.

"Never mind. Your face says it all." He stood, holding his hand out to help her up. "Will you let me take you somewhere else? Don't worry, it's basically a lawn with a lone tree here and there. Most of the trees are way off in the distance."

She put her hand in his—strong, comforting—and rose. "Where is it?"

"City Park. I want to show you the lake. It's the least-threatening place I can think of around here. It might give you a different impression of the area."

"City Park? It still exists?" A delicious buzz spread through her chest. "Tell me it's the same one that was here fifty years ago."

He shot her a quizzical look. "Yeah, why?"

Could it be possible she'd find the spot she'd heard about so many times from Mimi? "My grandfather proposed to my grandmother at City Park. It's one of the reasons I moved here."

"Just one of the reasons, huh?" His blue eyes twinkled. "I wonder if you'll tell me the others."

She doubted she'd tell Bryan the other reasons she'd tucked in her heart.

A place where dreams come true. The store. Friends. Maybe a husband down the line. Babies. Definitely babies.

A thread of hope wrapped around her soul. Bryan watched a hawk flying above them. The sharp planes of his jaw displayed the determined lift of his chin.

Opening the store would be enough for now. Wanting too much too soon would be asking for trouble.

Jade waved in the direction of the parking lot. "What are we waiting for?"

* * *

Ten minutes later Bryan hopped out of his black truck, jogged to the passenger's side and opened the door for Jade. A wide expanse of lawn dotted with picnic tables stretched before them. Branches of a weeping willow tree swept the ground, and in the distance, the lake appeared gray under the overcast sky. He hoped coming here would make her a little less tense.

He also hoped she hadn't minded him prying earlier. Bryan usually accepted when people said they didn't want to discuss something. After all, he didn't volunteer to air his soiled past, but when Jade said she didn't want to talk about whatever happened, curiosity started eating at him.

What had happened to the little seven-year-old green-eyed girl that still had the power to make her lips turn white and her lungs seize at the thought of entering the woods?

Whatever it was, it couldn't be good.

"Not the best day for the lake." He helped her down, shutting the door behind her. "It's usually turquoise with silver shining off it. It's still something, though, don't you think?"

"It's beautiful. I haven't had time to explore the town yet." Her cheeks glowed as she pointed. "Oh, is that the gazebo?"

"Want to see it?"

"Yes! Is it new? Or has it been here long?"

"It's been there ever since I can remember. Even made it through the tornado two years ago. Half the town was leveled, but not this park."

"A tornado? How awful. Were you affected?"

"Oh, it affected me." He strolled beside her. "Libby and Jake's wedding was scheduled for the next day, but they had to postpone it. The tornado destroyed Uncle Joe's Restaurant where their reception was being held. My sister Claire and Jake's brother, Reed, were trapped inside. But it turned out okay. I now have two brothers-in-law, Jake and Reed."

"You have a big family."

"Tell me about it." He loved his family, but sometimes he wondered if there had been a mistake on God's part. They were all exuberant. Nothing like him.

"I'm an only child." They reached the gazebo, but Jade didn't go inside. She pointed to an old, stately beech tree. "I think that's it!"

"What's what?"

She ran to it, bending her neck back to view the dark gray trunk where spring leaves waved from branches. Her fingers trailed the bark as she circled it. "I'm looking for a carving."

"You might be looking for a while." Hundreds of carvings had survived the years. He'd never marked the tree—didn't care for permanent displays for anyone to mock—but most of his friends had.

"It's supposed to be a heart with *F* plus *M* inside."

He searched for hearts. "What do the letters stand for?"

"Frank and Mimi." Her bright face popped out from behind the trunk. "He proposed to her here."

"Mimi was her real name? I thought it was her nickname, like Grandma or Nana." No wonder Jade beamed, touching the tree. He wanted to find the carving for her.

"Yeah, I always called her Mimi. I'm not sure why."

He searched the lower portion. Bryan craned his neck, hoping he'd missed something. "Are you sure this is the one?"

The sparkles in Jade's eyes disappeared as she put her

chin on her fist. "I don't know. Mimi always said it was a tall tree close to the gazebo with the lake shimmering behind them."

This one must be it, but he didn't see the markings. "It would have been a long time ago."

"Maybe we're not looking high enough." Jade peered up.

"That's not how it works. Trees grow upward from the tips of the branches, and the trunks thicken as they age. The carving won't be higher."

"Oh." Jade's lower lip pushed out. "I guess this isn't it."

A thin layer of moss on the bark caught Bryan's eye. He brushed it away with his hand. "Check this out."

Jade flew to his side. "Oh!" She covered her mouth, and her shining eyes met his. *Whoa.* Her delight was doing something to his pulse. He backed up two steps.

"That's it," her voice cracked. "It's really there. You found it. Thank you."

His chest expanded. How did she do that? Make him feel eight feet tall over something so minor?

Jade traced the faded heart, the letters, and sighed. "Dreams do come true."

A romantic. Bryan curled his fingertips inward until the skin pinched. What dream did Jade want to come true?

The store, of course.

Maybe more. Maybe she wanted a guy to carve their initials in a tree.

Too bad he wasn't a make-it-permanent, let-the-whole-world-see kind of guy anymore.

"I'm glad you found it," he said, not meeting her eyes.

So he was attracted to her. Big deal. He'd been attracted to several women since Abby left, but he'd reminded himself what was at stake. Technically, God forgave him for signing the divorce papers, but how could Bryan knowingly put himself in that situation again?

He wouldn't. He'd had his mistakes flaunted all around town when Abby's ex arrived and made house calls to their apartment for a full week while Bryan went off to work in obliviousness.

Everyone in Lake Endwell knew she cheated on him.

Everyone knew she left Bryan for another man.

And the town busybodies talked about it for months.

Jade was taking pictures of the carvings with her phone.

She was all alone in town, afraid of the very things he considered amazing. This afternoon proved she couldn't handle his class, but he couldn't just leave her to wade through her problems alone.

An idea formed. One that made him queasy.

He wanted her to see Lake Endwell through his eyes.

Lord, don't ask me to do that. It's too big a risk.

"Bryan?" Jade asked, a gentle smile on her lips. "Thanks for taking me here."

Uh-oh.

It might be okay. He was older, wiser, and hopefully, he'd be moving soon. He wouldn't be around to see who snatched Jade up and carved her initials in this beech tree.

"Sure." He rubbed the back of his neck, uncertain how to broach the subject. "Um, I don't think you're ready for my class."

The light in her eyes snuffed out.

"But," he continued, "I want to help. Why don't we keep meeting on Sunday afternoons? We can work through the rest of those therapy steps."

"What?" Jade scrunched her nose. Seagulls noisily landed a few yards away.

"Well, you're new here, and I don't want to worry about you passing out at a picnic." His smile teased, but she couldn't muster any enthusiasm. Why would he offer that? Either he felt sorry for her or it was his way of letting her know he was interested. She'd rather have him feel sorry for her. Less complicated that way.

"What would you get out of it?" she asked. "I'm not your responsibility."

"I don't need to get anything out of it."

"No." She shook her head. "I'll be fine. I can work through those steps on my own. You've already done so much."

His frown and the way he crossed his arms over his chest assured her she'd offended him, although she wasn't sure how.

"I've barely done a thing."

"Yes, you have. I've been in Evergreen Park twice in two days, which is twice more than I expected in such a short amount of time. And you found this." She flourished her hand to the tree.

"Are you really going to work through the steps on your own?" He narrowed his eyes.

"I can't ask you to give up all your free time."

"A few hours a week?" He scoffed. "It wouldn't be much. What's the real issue?"

She couldn't take him up on the offer, although it appealed to her. Her own personal outdoor expert—and a gorgeous one at that—patiently helping her get used to the woods? Who wouldn't want it? But she'd owe him, and owing meant strings, strings she was unwilling to tie if it meant he'd cut them later.

"I don't know. I have a lot on my plate with opening the store and everything."

Bryan seemed to see right through her. "If I told you something, would you keep it confidential?"

She nodded, hoping it wasn't going to make her life more difficult.

"I applied for a position in Ontario. It's a corporate retreat, and I'd be one of their outdoor instructors. But to get an interview, I need to prove I'm experienced. The human resources director wants to see logs of my classes. Hours taught, number of students. That sort of thing."

He was *moving*? Jade tried to pay attention as the information raced through her brain. She should be thrilled, but disappointment overrode her previous thoughts. His offer wasn't out of pity *or* attraction. "So you basically need to write down our hours and what we do?"

"Yeah. Their hiring process starts in June. It would give us five to seven weeks. I think we could make a lot of headway in getting over your fear."

All her reasons for declining fled. All but one. He might be moving, but the attraction she felt was very real. Could she keep it under control for a month or two?

"I don't know." She shrugged, wanting to say *yes*, knowing she should say *no*.

"It would help me out."

That sealed it. In twenty-four hours, Bryan had done nothing but help her and make her feel at home. The least she could do was return the favor. "I'll pay you."

"You're not paying me."

"Why not?" She could justify the whole thing more if she paid him.

"That's not why I asked, and frankly, I don't need the money."

Of course he didn't. She wanted to think about it, to talk herself out of it, but she took a deep breath. Bryan could help her with her phobia. He had an uncanny knack for distracting her when she felt overwhelmed. She'd just have to protect her heart.

"I'll find a way to pay you back."

"If something comes up, you'll be the first to know."

Chapter Four

"Who was with you at the park today? Sally mentioned driving by and seeing you with a girl."

Bryan stacked two empty pizza boxes on the kitchen counter and waved for Dad to join him in the living room. He hadn't considered the rumor mill when he'd offered to help Jade. In small towns like this, gossip spread as quickly as dandelion seeds on a windy day.

"You? With a girl?" Sam snorted and tapped his fingertips together. "It's about time."

"How did you meet her?" Dad asked.

"Does Aunt Sally ever stay home?" Hoping they would drop the subject, Bryan sprawled out on the couch. The Detroit Tigers were playing tonight, and the lingering scent of Italian spices filled the air. "Shouldn't she be watching one of those *Real Housewives* shows she complains about?"

"I thought she gave up on them." Dad rocked back in the recliner, propping his feet up on the footrest. "Didn't she switch to some show with a single guy?"

"*The Bachelor*?" Sam asked.

"Yeah, that's the one." Dad nodded. "Bryan, you going to tell us or not?"

He clearly wasn't getting out of it. "Jade is the student I mentioned. She can't make the Saturday morning classes, so I'm tutoring her on Sundays instead. That's it." If he hadn't given Jade his word, he'd march over to her apartment and come up with an excuse to get out of spending Sundays with her. But he'd offered, and he kept his commitments. Well, all but one. The most important one. His marriage.

The doorbell rang. No one ever rang doorbells in Lake Endwell.

Dad reached the door first, and a huge beast of a dog plunged inside. A pink leash trailed the giant.

What in the world?

Lucy Bloomhall, a data-entry clerk at one of Bryan's dealerships, followed the dog into the living room. Lucy carried a large tote bag. Her blond hair was windblown, and her face had a dazed appearance.

"Here you go, Mr. Sheffield." She smiled at Bryan, and her gaze lingered on Sam. She blushed. "Thanks again for taking her. I don't know what I would have done if you'd turned me down. My parents wanted to help, you know, but Mom's allergic, plus they're traveling to Montana in a few weeks. I couldn't find anyone to watch Teeny for me."

He scratched his chin, vaguely remembering telling Lucy her dog would be fine while she spent part of her final college semester studying in Spain. Something to do with art. Or architecture. He couldn't remember, except it started with an _A_. She'd been frantic when she flew into his office last week, and he'd been poring over the profit and loss statements.

"Her bowls are in there, and she loves the Kong toy. You won't have any trouble with her. Oh, I have more food in my car. I'll bring it in." Lucy swiveled and practically sprinted across the porch.

The dog had jumped onto the couch. Slobber dripped from her mouth to the leather cushions.

"What. Is. This?" Sam stood in the middle of the room, gesturing at the dog, at Bryan and back at the dog.

"Looks like a Saint Bernard. She's a beauty." Dad bent to scratch behind her ears. She licked his face. The pooch had white and brown markings with black fur around her eyes. A noise outside startled her. As she leaped off the couch, her tail caught a lamp, flipping it to the ground with a crash before she escaped out the front door.

Bryan flew after her. "Catch it!" He made it to the bottom porch step, but Lucy gripped the leash and was attempting to drag the dog back to the house. Bryan jogged to her. "Let me."

Adoration glowed from her hazel eyes. "Thanks again. I know Teeny will be in good hands. My flight leaves tonight. Oh, before I forget—I wrote down all my contact information. It's in my purse."

Teeny lurched ahead, almost yanking free from Bryan's hand. Strong dog. He didn't want this responsibility, but— he looked at Lucy as she rummaged through her purse— could he really break her heart and make her find someone else when her flight was leaving in a few hours?

His life kept getting more complicated. And he didn't like it. Not one bit.

She beamed, handing him the paper. Girlie handwriting. Her *i*'s were dotted with little circles. "If it's not too much trouble, would you text me a picture now and then? I'm going to miss this girl." She wrapped her arms around Teeny. When Lucy straightened, tears glistened in her eyes.

Tears? He didn't do tears. He'd say about anything to prevent her from crying. "I'll take good care of her."

Lucy blinked a few times and smiled. "She's eight months old. A puppy, really. Oh, her obedience classes are on Wednesday nights at Perfect Puppy, but don't feel as if you have to take her or anything. They're paid for if you want to go, though. I better leave before I start bawling. Thanks again."

"Enjoy yourself," Bryan said gruffly. "And study hard."

"I will." She waved and trotted back to her car. "See you the end of July."

The end of July? He wouldn't be here. If he got an interview with Blue Mountain Retreat, passed the skills test and got hired, the director expected him to be ready to teach by July. Who would take care of this hulking, slobbery mess of a mutt? Bryan stared at Teeny, who gazed up at him with big chocolate eyes. Drool dripped from her mouth. She kind of looked like she was smiling.

"Well, Teeny, looks as if you're staying with us. Come on." He tugged on her leash, and she followed him into the house.

"No way." Sam shook his head with his arms locked straight out in front of him. "We are not keeping that thing. I don't care what you told Lucy. You should have run it by me first."

Bryan used his shoulder to shut the front door and unhooked the leash from Teeny's hot-pink collar. "I didn't realize…"

"You didn't realize I should have some say in living with—" Sam had a crazed look about him as he gestured to Teeny "—this mutant of a dog? I've seen ponies smaller than her."

"She is large." Bryan ran his thumb over his lips. Living with Sam's dramatics could be annoying at times. Like now. It was a dog. Big deal.

"I like her." Dad ruffled the fur on her head. "Reminds me of Penny. Remember the golden lab, Bryan?"

"Yeah, Penny was a good dog."

Sam threw his hands in the air. "We're not talking about Penny. We're talking about Teeny. The thing's been here five minutes and managed to leave pools of spit on every seat in the room."

Bryan gave the space the once-over. *Huh.* Sam was right. Teeny's drool lay in puddles throughout the room.

"And you saw how it rocketed out the front door. How are we going to control the thing? We'll never be able to keep that monster inside. It's going to shed everywhere. It'll stink. Probably already does. I can't go to work covered in dog hair."

Teeny plopped at Dad's feet, licked her chops twice and looked right at home.

"Lucy said something about instructions." Bryan poked through the tote bag. Stuffed animals, bags of dog treats, a big rubber ball with knobs all over it and—there, at the bottom—a sheet of paper with Lucy's loopy writing. "Here it is. Yeah, Wednesdays are obedience classes if you want to take her. She needs a walk every day. A scoop of food in the morning, one at night. No big deal."

"If *I* want to take her?" Sam jabbed his thumb into his chest. "You're the one who's taking her."

"I'm not taking her." Him? Alone at a dog obedience class? People around town had enough to titter about. They didn't need to see his ineptness with this dog, too. He had no experience training an animal, and he had enough to worry about between running his dealerships and trying to get more students to his class.

Silence stretched as Bryan locked eyes with Sam.

Finally, Sam made a chopping gesture. "If Teeny doesn't follow the house rules, she's out of here."

Bryan had to wonder what the house rules were and where Teeny would go. "If it's going to throw you into cardiac arrest, I'll move into Granddad's cottage."

"What? No. If anyone is living there, it's going to be me."

He took a deep breath. There was no reason for Sam to move out, not when Bryan only had a few months left in town. But he couldn't explain. Not yet. Not with so many uncertainties.

He would tell his family about moving to Canada *after* he landed the job.

"Would you give Teeny a chance before doing anything drastic?" Bryan asked Sam.

"Fine. But don't ask me to walk, feed or pick up after her." Sam swiveled and stomped to his bedroom, slamming the door behind him.

"I've got to get going, but call me if you need help with this girl." Dad let himself out.

Teeny hopped onto the couch, spreading her body across the whole thing, and fell asleep, her chin resting on her enormous white paws. Maybe Dad would take care of Teeny when Bryan moved.

He frowned. He had a lot of unanswered questions to work out. Like who would manage his dealerships in his absence. They were a lucrative part of Sheffield Auto. Tommy and Sam could split them, but Tommy was busy enough with the impending arrival of his baby, and Sam was still learning the ropes of his own dealership. Bryan's assistant manager could be promoted to run both, but only if his dad and brothers approved.

Other than that, this bungalow was paid for, so Sam could continue living here if he wanted. And Dad would probably watch Teeny the last few weeks of Lucy's semester.

What about Jade?

Bryan grabbed the laptop from the desk in his bedroom and set it on his lap as the Tigers took the field. Maybe if Jade knew more about the trees native to the area, she'd relax a little. He typed names of trees into the search engine. An image of her shining face came to mind.

He'd do his duty. Help her. And move on to Canada. Everything would work out fine.

He just had to trust God to take care of the details.

"I'm desperate." Bryan ignored Teeny panting next to him in a rare moment of calmness at Evergreen Park. "I can't teach Jade and watch the dog."

"Call Dad or Claire. I told you, I'm working on reports." Sam spun on his heel and marched in the direction of his truck. Halfway there, he turned back. "By the way, that beast used my new work shoes as chew toys last night."

"She's just a puppy." Why did Bryan even waste his breath? And why was Teeny making a mess of everything? Over a seven-day period, she'd torn a gaping hole in the recliner, chewed chunks out of every coffee table leg, permanently stained the leather couch with her slobber and she'd eaten two socks, a television remote and, apparently, Sam's new work shoes. *Terrific.*

He could *not* leave the dog alone at home. There would be no home left. Teeny destroyed everything she came into contact with.

Bryan led her to the pavilion to wait for Jade. Last night, he'd called every family member and friend he could think of to watch the dog, but no one was available. He toyed with the idea of texting Aunt Sally, but he wasn't that big of a jerk. The animal would mow down his puny aunt.

He patted Teeny's furry head. "Looks like you're staying with me today. I hope Jade doesn't mind dogs."

Jade's red car pulled into a parking spot. Bryan stood straighter as she approached. Her movements revealed her tension, and the sparkle he'd associated with her when they weren't near trees was MIA. Her T-shirt showed a steaming mug of coffee with the words Bring Me My Latte.

"You like coffee?" Bryan tightened his grip on the leash. Teeny stood, her tail wagging, and let out two low woofs. "Down, girl."

"Couldn't live without it." She nodded at the dog. "Who is this?"

"Teeny."

"Really? Hey, Teeny." Jade held her closed fist in front of the dog's nose. Teeny sniffed it, gazing up at her with hopeful eyes. Jade massaged behind both of her fluffy ears. "You're a big cutie, you know that?"

"She's a pain."

"This bundle of sunshine? I don't believe it." Jade continued to stroke her fur, and Teeny took the opportunity to lick her face. "Eww, but thank you for the kiss, even if it was wet and sloppy."

She gestured for Bryan to hand her the leash. He hesitated. "She's still an untrained puppy."

"Don't worry. I may be petite, but I can handle a big dog."

That made one of them. He handed it to her. She held the leash loosely in her hand and continued to lavish Teeny with attention.

"I'm glad someone can, because my brother and I are hopeless at it. I'm watching her for a few months."

"She's not yours?" A hint of color returned to Jade's cheeks, and her arms moved more loosely as she petted Teeny.

"One of my employees is studying abroad. She couldn't find anyone to watch the dog." Bryan leaned his arm against the pavilion post. "How are you settling in?"

"Pretty good. I'm working on the store layout. The apartment is unpacked as much as I can get it. I'm going to have to break down and buy some curtains soon, though."

"You still don't have curtains?" Bryan frowned. Lake Endwell boasted few crimes, but he didn't like to think of her windows inviting prying eyes. "If you need help putting anything up, let me know."

His phone dinged. *Dad. I can be there in 5 if you need me to take Teeny.*

The tension in Bryan's neck eased. One problem solved. He texted Dad back to thank him, then slipped his phone back into his pocket. "Mind waiting a few minutes? My dad's coming for the dog."

"Aw, that's too bad." Jade wound the leash around her hand. "I like her. She's adorable."

"Tell that to my brother Sam. He's had at least six tantrums since she arrived."

Jade laughed. "How old is Sam?"

"Twenty-five. Too old to be acting like a baby, if you ask me."

"Did anyone show up to your class yesterday?"

"Yes." He moved out of the pavilion to stand in the sun, and Jade joined him. "Aunt Sally recruited two members of the Ladies' Aid at church. Miss Ada is ninety-two years old. I think she might have known more about edible berries than I do. Linda is her seventy-year-old daughter."

"Why am I sensing a problem?" Her eyes twinkled as she caught her lower lip between her teeth. The sunshine glinted off her hair.

"They were temporary students. Could only make it to class yesterday. They're driving to California to stay with a cousin for the summer. Honestly, they were fun to hang out with. Linda showed me how to make tea out of sassafras roots."

Jade cocked her head, a huge smile on her face. "You are full of surprises, Bryan."

He tucked her comment away. She didn't seem to think it odd he enjoyed the company of two elderly women who knew as much, if not more, about plants and trees than he did.

"So what's the plan today?" Jade asked.

He unzipped his backpack and pulled out the stack of papers he'd printed last night. Thumbing through, he checked them, then handed the packet to her. "Knowledge is power."

"Okaaay." She stretched the word as she scanned the top sheet.

"I'm giving you a lesson on the most common trees in our area and why we need them." Bryan couldn't help but believe her fear would be tamed if she knew more about North American forests.

"And this will help how?"

"Would you hate an oak if you know it's an owl's home, a starling's lookout, a safe spot for rabbits and a way for a deer to find its mate?"

"Wait, what?" Her eyes grew wide. "I don't think I want to know about the deer thing."

He chuckled. The crunch of footsteps diverted his

attention. Dad trekked toward them. Thick silver hair topped his permanently tan face with laugh lines crinkling around the Sheffield blue eyes. He wore his usual— baggy jeans, work boots and a Carhartt jacket.

"Thanks for coming, Dad." Bryan took the leash from Jade and handed it to him. Teeny jumped up, placing her huge paws on Dad's chest.

"Easy does it, Teeny." Dad pushed her paws down and snapped his fingers for her to sit. She didn't comply, but at least she stayed on all fours, her tail wagging and her tongue lolling.

"Jade, this is my dad, Dale Sheffield. Dad, this is Jade Emerson."

"Nice to meet you." Dad shook Jade's hand, then turned back to Bryan. "I'll get this dog out of your hair. You can pick her up at my house later."

"Thanks."

Teeny spotted a chipmunk and vaulted in its direction, almost jerking Dad off his feet. But he dug his boots into the ground and scolded her until she resumed an easy trot by his side.

Bryan drew his shoulders back. The dog was taken care of. Now to take care of Jade.

Wait. Not take care of her. *Teach* her.

"I'm giving you a crash course about trees. Hardwoods, conifers, you name it."

"Sounds good." One side of her mouth quirked upward. "But I draw the line at deer habits."

Bryan laughed. At least she had a go-to attitude about dealing with her fear. Abby had refused to let him show her the beauty of the area. Hiking, camping and the outdoors weren't her thing. She'd made reservations at upscale restaurants an hour away. Hosted theme parties when he preferred watching sports with the guys. He didn't blame her for not enjoying the things he did, but it hadn't helped the strain on their already rocky marriage.

He hoped Jade wouldn't be bored out of her mind. One good thing? He didn't feel tongue-tied around her the way he did around many women. If someone had told him two weeks ago he'd be spending Sunday afternoons with a beautiful girl and actually enjoying himself, he never would have believed them.

But what did it matter? He had a job to land in Canada, and helping Jade was just a brief perk.

What would it be like if he stayed?

He couldn't go down that road. This was temporary. It had to be.

Chapter Five

Jade climbed another rung of the ladder and stretched on her tiptoes to cover a purple smudge on the ceiling. Her paintbrush just reached. She swiped over the mistake with white paint and stepped down to survey the room. The space glowed. The colors, lighting, the open feel and size of the store—everything was exactly as she'd envisioned it.

Yesterday had gone better than she could have hoped. Bryan had been the definition of patience as he led her around the perimeter of the park, pointing out different species of trees and explaining why they were important. She'd even stood with him at the blue path entrance again, and this time she didn't feel as panicky.

She wished she could repay him somehow. The printout of trees must have taken hours to put together. And spending time outside with him was helping her relax. She might even be able to attempt driving out of town soon. Zooming past trees in her car didn't seem as threatening as it had been when she first arrived.

Jade tapped the lid back on the paint can and wiped her hands on a paper towel. The electrician she hired had installed recessed lighting and additional electric outlets behind the counter and in the back workspace. The display tables were set to arrive tomorrow, but her big purchases—the screen-printing press, T-shirt printer and the engraver—wouldn't be here until next week. She'd taken care of the remaining business paperwork, including following up on her city business license, getting her state business number and filling out the forms for the federal government.

With her hands against her lower back, she stretched, noticing movement outside.

Two women stopped in front of the window. Libby waved and gestured to the door. A burst of happiness warmed Jade's heart seeing Libby's smiling face. She ushered them inside.

"We brought you dinner." Libby trailed a petite older woman with bleached blond hair and kind, yet sharp, blue eyes. "This is Aunt Sally."

"Well, look at that. You're fun size, like me." Sally's bright pink lips kicked into a grin.

Jade chuckled. They *were* about the same height and build.

Sally continued. "It's good to finally meet you. Jules Reichert told me you were opening a T-shirt shop here. I'd love to have new shirts made up to sell at the restaurant. Our old ones finally sold out, but I should have tossed them. They had big, bubble letters like in the eighties. Tacky."

"I'd be happy to sketch designs for you." Jade closed the door behind them. Aunt Sally was her type of lady. Very Vegas-like with glittery, dangly fish-shaped earrings, heavy mascara, tight jeans and a royal blue sweatshirt with Lake Endwell Wildcats in white lettering.

Sally set a large paper bag on the floor. "We saw you working in here earlier and figured you could use some food. You can put it in the fridge until you're ready to eat."

"Really? Thank you." Jade wanted to offer them a place to sit, but the hardwood floors were empty of furniture.

"I love the colors you chose." Libby strolled along the perimeter, eyeing the cream walls broken up by an eggplant accent wall. "When do you think you'll open?"

Jade grabbed the ceiling paint. "Pretty soon. Early May. I'll be making up samples this week. Just waiting for my machines to come in. I'm excited to get back into it."

"Did you have a shop in Las Vegas?" Sally asked.

"No," Jade said. "I had a stressful job in advertising. But in college I worked for an amazing T-shirt designer. Learned everything from her." She set the can down behind the counter near the back wall. Sally followed her, stopping in front of the counter.

"What are you planning on selling?"

"My base products are T-shirts, custom tote bags, sweatshirts and yoga pants. I'm researching a companion line to sell, like candles, lotions. Or cute purses and scarves. I'll probably test different items before making any permanent decisions."

"Good idea." Sally leaned on the counter. "Libby told me you're taking Bryan's class. How are you liking it?"

Jade ripped off a sheet of paper towel and bent to wipe a paint drip from the can before it hit the floor. "Well, I'm not exactly taking the class, but Bryan is teaching me on Sundays. He's very patient."

And nice. And really, really cute. But she wasn't saying that to his relatives.

"Patient." Sally grinned. "Bryan is one of the few Sheffields to get the trait."

Jade tossed the paper towel into a plastic grocery bag she set out for trash.

"We all know I didn't get it." Libby joined them. "Claire and Bryan are the only ones in our family with patience. That ginormous dog is testing both Sam's and Bryan's patience a little too much, if you ask me. Lucy paid for obedience classes. Bryan needs to take the dog."

"I know," Sally said. "I know."

Libby extended her hand, fingers spread. "I keep telling Sam to chill out, but I don't blame him for being mad. I mean, Bryan took the dog in, and he should be responsible for making it mind."

"Are you talking about the adorable Saint Bernard, Teeny?" Jade wrapped one arm around her waist and propped her elbow on it. Her cheek fell against her palm.

"Yes." Libby nodded. "Please tell me she hasn't destroyed anything of yours."

"No, no." Jade laughed. "Bryan had her with him yesterday. I love dogs, especially big dogs."

Sally turned her head and exchanged an unspoken communication with Libby. Jade remembered sharing similar looks with her best friend in high school. The automatic understanding would flash invisible, yet so real, between them.

A drop of sadness rippled through her chest. The past two years had revolved around working during the day and caring for Mimi at night. Jade had lost touch with her best friend years ago, and her other friends had transferred across the country. It had been a long time since Jade shared secrets or had fun.

"You love dogs. Big dogs." Libby's matter-of-fact tone set off tiny alarms in Jade's brain.

"I do." Jade could see where Libby's mind was going. *Why not?* Bryan wouldn't let her pay him for their Sunday lessons. She lifted a shoulder. "Maybe I could take Teeny to her classes."

"Bryan does need help." Sally nodded, speaking slowly. "But that's too much to ask. You've got your hands full here."

"Like I said, I love dogs. It wouldn't be a big deal."

Libby shook her head. "We couldn't ask you to do that."

"It would make me feel better." Jade spread her arms wide, opening her hands. "Bryan won't let me pay him for the private lessons."

"You don't have to pay him, hon." Sally waved. "Wait, if you're not taking his class on Saturdays anymore… Well, Libby, looks like I'll have to recruit students again."

"Why is he so on fire about this class, anyway?" Libby flicked her fingernail. "He's taking it a little too seriously if you ask me."

"It's good for him." Sally shook her head. "It's getting him out and about."

"Well, I already pinned his fliers at the grocery store, the donut shop and the library."

Jade studied her shoes. She knew the reason Bryan offered the class. He clearly hadn't been kidding when he said it was a secret. Uneasiness crept up her spine. She'd promised to keep it confidential, but why was he keeping his plans from his family?

She shifted her weight from one foot to the other. "He told me a couple ladies from his church came to class Saturday."

"Ada and Louise." Sally nodded. "Too bad they won't be around anymore. If worse comes to worst, I'll try to talk Sam into going. Or Joe and I could pop in."

"If Sam won't, I'll take one for the team." Libby straightened her shoulders and lifted her chin as though she faced a fiery furnace. "Don't get me wrong, Jade. It's not that I don't love Bryan, but tripping through the forest isn't my idea of fun."

Jade liked Libby even more after that declaration.

"I'll get the word out." Sally drummed her nails on the counter. "So, Jade, you don't mind going with Bryan to the dog obedience classes?"

Jade sputtered. Go *with* Bryan? That hadn't been her intention. "Oh, I was thinking I would take the dog by myself."

"I like your enthusiasm, but that wouldn't help him, because he needs to know how to make Teeny mind."

She had a point.

Libby made a tsking sound. "None of us can watch her until she stops destroying everything she sees."

"Why can't one of you go with him?" The thought of spending time with Teeny appealed, but Jade shouldn't spend more time with the dog's gorgeous caretaker.

"We would, hon, we would." Sally let out a pitiful sigh. "Libby, here, is finishing her final semester of college and has class. I'm on duty at the restaurant Wednesdays. Dale and Reed have been working overtime building more homes in the subdivision. Claire gets home from the zoo late. And Sam…"

"Hates the dog?" Jade asked.

Libby and Sally averted their eyes. Bryan *had* seemed desperate to get rid of the dog yesterday. "It would be weird for me to contact Bryan and out of the blue say, 'Hey, I'm going to dog training with you.'"

"You're right. It would be weird. Don't worry. I'll call him right now." Sally whipped out her phone, swiped the screen and held it to her ear. "Hi, honey. Listen, we're at Jade's, and she's willing to go to obedience class with you Wednesday night." Her face twisted in displeasure as she listened to Bryan. "No, no. We asked her to go… Because that dog needs to be trained."

So much for that. Jade glanced at Libby, who lifted a finger and mouthed, "Wait."

"Sam told me about the classes." Sally gazed at the ceiling. "I know…Yes, of course I know. Look, Jade likes the dog, and frankly, she's the only one I know besides your dad who does. Why not try it at least?" She tapped the back of the phone with her finger. "Good. Okay, then, hon…Yep. I'll tell her. Love you."

Sally grinned. "He'll pick you up at six thirty Wednesday night."

Jade fought to keep from frowning. The way Sally said it made it sound like a date.

"Do you have Bryan's cell number?" Libby asked.

"Nope."

"Well, give me yours, and I'll text it to you." She held her hand out. "Add me to your contacts, too. I have a friend who makes custom jewelry. You might want to talk to her. Maybe her pieces would work in here."

Jade told her the number as Libby typed it into her phone.

"We appreciate this, Jade." Libby brought her hands together, her eyes shining. "Let's get together soon. Text me anytime."

Bryan parked his truck in front of Jade's store Wednesday evening. Teeny drooled all over the passenger seat as she stared out the front window. "Well, I'd ask you not to embarrass me tonight, but I know you will."

After teaching Jade Sunday, he'd driven out to Granddad's cottage to think. Jade's teasing manner had taken the edge off his need to escape Lake Endwell. And that wouldn't do. He had no future with Jade or any woman, and he needed to remember it.

Last night he'd spent hours researching wildlife in the Blue Mountain region of Canada. Next on his list? Native birds in Ontario. When he got the call in a month or two, he wanted to be as ready as possible to impress the director.

Teeny licked his hand. Why had Aunt Sally asked Jade to go to these dumb classes with him? Another tight spot to be in, all because of his family.

He got out and walked up the sidewalk. Sometimes his family was great. But when his sister and aunt put their cute little noses in his personal business...well, he didn't like it. Not one bit.

Bryan jogged up the stairs to Jade's apartment and rapped on her door twice. She opened it, and his breath caught. Soft light filtered around her flowing, shiny hair. Her green eyes reminded him of spring grass, and her teeth gleamed in a wide smile.

He'd never seen a smile like that. His heartbeat raced as if a gun had gone off. Every thought in his head went on break. She stepped forward, brushing his arm in the process. Her perfume—something exotic, feminine—wreathed around him.

"Hi." Her tone had a bounce to it. "I hear Teeny needs some rules."

"She sure does." His voice cracked. He cleared his throat.

"Well, let's go train that dog."

She skipped down the steps and made baby faces at Teeny through the passenger window.

"Give me a minute," Bryan said. "I'll hold her so you can get in."

He climbed into the driver's seat, grabbed Teeny's collar and urged her to the backseat, but she didn't move. Jade opened the door.

"Wait!" Certain the dog would leap out and run, Bryan gripped her collar. But Jade stood tall, crowding Teeny until the mutt was forced to hop in the backseat. She took a tissue from her purse and wiped the drool off the leather. Bryan blinked. "How did you do that?"

"Do what?" She wadded the tissue and looked around for somewhere to put it. He held his palm out. She handed him the tissue.

"Keep her from jumping out."

"Oh, that." She waved. "No biggie. My old boss always brought her Great Dane into the shop with her. We had all kinds of tricks to keep Baby from escaping."

"Baby? What's with the names for these big dogs?" He jerked his thumb backward. "This one should be named Hercules or Queen Kong or something."

Jade laughed. "Queen Kong. I like it."

He shifted into Drive and asked her about the store. She filled him in on the furniture still in boxes that came in yesterday.

"Your sister and aunt raved about your car dealerships." She shifted to face him. Her creamy skin looked sun-kissed, and his mouth went dry. "How did you get into your line of work?"

"Sheffield Auto is a family business." His throat was crusty as two-day-old bread. "Granddad started it, then Dad took over. Now Tommy, Sam and I run it."

"Impressive," she said. "Your family seems close."

"We are." He kept his focus straight ahead. No sense sending his blood pressure off the charts staring at her pretty face. "Tell me about yours. Was it just you and Mimi all those years? What happened to your parents?"

"My parents divorced when I was three. They decided

Mimi would raise me. Mom's a cancer researcher for the World Health Organization in France, and Dad's a heart surgeon for the Mayo Clinic in Phoenix."

"Demanding jobs." He frowned. Why would anyone send their kid, practically a baby, to live with someone else? He wanted to ask, but it was none of his business. "I'm surprised you didn't go into medicine."

"So were my parents." Her curt laugh didn't sound mirthful.

He darted a glance her way. "I take it they were disappointed?"

A tight smile accompanied her shrug. "When aren't they disappointed?"

Bryan frowned. It didn't seem possible anyone could be disappointed in someone as dazzling as Jade.

"They both have demanding careers. I guess they expected the same from me."

"Starting your own business is demanding." Bryan stole a peek at her and wished he hadn't. She looked beautiful and...sad.

Her halfhearted chuckle yanked at his heart. "Tell that to them. I rarely talk to my father. He paid for my college, though, and I'm thankful for that. Maybe my parents did me a favor handing me over to Mimi when they did. Better her than a nanny or boarding school."

He rolled into the long, winding driveway of Perfect Puppy, the doggy day care and boarding service at the edge of town. Pressure built in his chest at the hurt in her eyes and the way she justified her parents' actions. He shouldn't judge. He'd better keep his mouth shut or he'd say something he'd regret, something like, *Your parents are jerks and should have their heads examined.*

He parked, pressing the brakes with more force than necessary. "Sorry."

At the entrance, Teeny pressed her nose against the glass door. Her tail hit the backs of Bryan's knees. He opened the door for Jade and fumbled to get Lucy's receipt out of his pocket. Jade took the leash from him. She nodded to a group of people with dogs of various sizes. "I'll take her over there while you straighten things out with the instructor."

"Do you think that's a good idea?" Bryan eyed the crowd. Teeny was so rambunctious.

"We'll be fine."

Against his better judgment, he let Jade leave. Bryan found DeeDee Matthews, the owner of Perfect Puppy, and mentioned Lucy's arrangement. Certain Teeny had destroyed something in the thirty seconds his back was turned, he dreaded having to find Jade. But when he looked in her direction, he exhaled. Jade stood near other owners while Teeny and a schnauzer greeted each other in doggy fashion.

"Let's get started." DeeDee clapped her hands.

As Jade transferred the leash to Bryan, her fingers brushed his in the process, distracting him. Teeny took the opportunity to charge across the open floor, the leash dragging behind her.

A hand grenade minus the pin dropped in Bryan's gut, but he ran after the dog. She'd lowered her front legs and barked at a Chihuahua trembling under its owner's chair.

Perfect. The brute was officially bullying a tiny, terrified dog.

"I'm sorry," he said quietly, and dragged—or tried to drag—Teeny to the other side of the room where Jade attempted to control her laughter. He didn't find anything funny about it.

DeeDee continued. "I'm glad so many of you could make it tonight. For those of you who are new, I'll share a quick rundown of our rules. The dogs remain on leash and at your side throughout the class. At the end of the session, we allow the dogs to greet one another, but they must remain on their leashes. We address behavior issues with a squirt of water." She held up a clear plastic spray bottle. "If you haven't purchased a clicker and treats, I have extras up here and you can pay me after class."

Jade elbowed Bryan's arm. "Do you have a clicker?"

He shook his head and leaned toward her. "No treats, either."

DeeDee led a small white poodle to the center of the room. "I'll be demonstrating with Izzy. Let's review how to get your dog to sit. Here's the sequence. Stand in front of your dog. Raise your hand, palm up, and say in a firm tone, 'Sit.' When your dog sits, click the clicker and feed her a treat."

DeeDee went through the steps with Izzy, who performed them easily right down to eating the treat after the click.

"Think we can get Teeny to do that?" Jade whispered.

"Not in ten years."

She chortled under her breath.

"You laugh now," he muttered. "But wait until Teeny eats the Chihuahua. No one will be laughing then."

"It looks like we can start," Jade said. "I'll go get the clicker and treats while you find a spot."

Bryan looked at Teeny. Teeny looked at him. He had a sinking sensation, like the time he stood too quickly in Granddad's fishing boat, lost his balance and fell into the lake.

"Here we are." Jade handed him a small blue box with a metal button that made a clicking sound when pressed. It fit in the palm of his hand. "Try it."

"What do I do first again?" Did he tell her to sit, raise his hand or give her a treat? It all seemed confusing.

"Um, raise your palm and say, 'Sit.'"

He did. Teeny wagged her tail and panted. He repeated the command. She ignored him.

"I think this dog is defective." He clicked the clicker. Teeny did nothing.

"Let me try." Jade held out her hand.

Bryan gave her the clicker and leash. He had no doubt she would tell Teeny to sit and the dog would obey. All the other dogs were sitting and gobbling up treats.

"Teeny, sit." Jade raised her palm. A line of drool dropped to the floor, but she didn't sit. "Maybe we have to push her bottom down so she knows what we want."

The fact Jade couldn't get the dog to obey either was like a flash of sunshine on a miserable day. He wasn't the only one bad at this.

Jade gave him the leash. "Here. You do the spiel again, and I'll press on her back."

Bryan went through the motions as Jade pressed lightly on Teeny's backside. Teeny sat.

"Hurry, click it!" Jade yelled.

He clicked the thing and handed Teeny a treat. He'd give her a handful if she'd listen to him.

"We did it!" Jade held her hand up for a high five, and Bryan slapped her palm.

"Yeah, but can we do it again?"

She grinned. "It's worth a try."

He commanded Teeny to sit. It took a few attempts, but by the end of the class, she was sitting regularly. When class let out, Bryan and Jade made their way to the truck. "Thanks for coming with me. I would be hopeless at this if you weren't here."

Her smile reached all the way to her eyes. "It's easier with a partner."

A partner. Something he'd longed for when he'd married Abby. Another dream he'd put to rest after she left.

Their feet crunched over the gravel on the way to his truck. "Teeny needs a lot more training before I can leave her alone. At least I have hope now."

"What happens when you leave her alone?" Jade took easy strides, her chin up and shoulders back. He liked seeing the relaxed, confident side of her.

"Sam nicknamed her Teeny the Destroyer."

Covering her mouth, she laughed. "She can't be that bad."

Bryan didn't say a word, just widened his eyes. The trees lining the parking lot had begun to flower with white and pink blossoms. The sweet scent of spring filled the air.

"Do you need me to watch her during your class on Saturday?"

"I couldn't ask you to do that." He tightened his hold on the leash.

"Why not?"

"She's big, untrained, and I worry she'd pull you off your feet."

Jade rolled her eyes. "I told you. I can handle a big dog. Bring her to the park. I'll take her around the lawn and study the trees you showed me. She probably needs a lot of exercise."

"I don't…"

"Bryan, I already feel bad you're helping me on Sundays. You won't let me pay you. Let me walk your dog during class this week."

Bryan had to say no. He was sliding into murky territory with Jade. Which wasn't smart, not after five years of frozen emotions.

"I'm going to try working through some of the therapy list on my own," she said. "Maybe with Teeny by my side, I could take a few steps on one of the paths."

Bryan opened the passenger door for her. He walked Teeny almost every day, and she lunged for birds and squirrels a few times, but he'd been able to control her. Maybe Jade *could* handle the dog. If it helped her overcome her fear, how could he refuse?

Late Friday morning, Jade cupped her hands around a cardboard cup of coffee and gazed out at the beauty before her. The sun spread happiness over City Park and laughed in silver glints off the lake. Pastel petals drifted to the ground. Jade wanted to scoop them up and fill a glass dish with their delicate beauty. It was nice, enjoying a product of trees for once. And hopefully today she'd get through step five of the exposure therapy worksheet she'd printed.

A worn path through the grass led to a wooded area in the distance. Far enough away from the gazebo to enjoy her coffee but close enough for her to hike over and work through the next item on the list.

The first four steps she'd conquered with Bryan. But step five involved moving a few feet into the forest while being aware of her feelings. Neither were strong suits of hers.

She sipped her coffee. She'd made a new daily ritual of exchanging small talk with Art Dunkirk, former owner of the Daily Donut. His fifty-year-old daughter, Marie, ran the shop now, but Art spent his mornings chugging coffee at the counter and harassing Marie, who sassed him but clearly loved him. Every morning at eight, Jade hopped onto the stool next to Art, ordered a large coffee to go and nibbled on a pastry while he filled her in on the gossip and history of Lake Endwell.

She'd stayed ten minutes longer than usual today. Dawdling. The task before her would surely throw her into a panic attack.

She didn't want to do step five.

Pulling her phone from her pocket, she sighed, then found the voice recording function. She figured saying her feelings out loud would be therapeutic.

After tossing her cup in the trash can, she clicked Record. "I'm in City Park. There's a grove of trees and dense brush to my left. I'm walking that way. Not feeling out of breath or shaky yet."

Geese honked overhead. They disappeared beyond the tree line.

"The air smells like the lake today but not in a bad way. It's clean, fragrant, hard to describe." Her footsteps crawled as she approached the grove of trees. "The ground isn't as soft here. Twigs and dirt are packed into the grass. Old weeds block the dirt path. I'll have to step on them to enter the woods."

She peered down at her running shoes. As rooted to the spot as the trunks before her.

"I'm starting to feel overwhelmed. I haven't gone inside, but I feel as if the trees are reaching for me, dragging me in where I don't want to go." She inhaled a deep, but shaky, breath. *Come on, Jade. Step five. You've got this.*

Her right foot crushed the weeds. Then her left.

And she was in the woods.

She heard nothing out of the ordinary, yet a roaring sound filled her head. Her throat tightened, and her pulse clobbered her temples. "I'm...I'm...scared," she whispered. A sudden movement in a clump of tall grass ahead made her jump with her hand to her chest. *Stupid squirrel.*

I can't do this.

Try. Come on. Just try.

Her head spun. She thrust her hand out, anchoring it to a tree trunk. She brought her phone up again. "Might pass out."

What was she supposed to be doing? What had the therapy site said to do?

Feelings. Be aware of feelings.

"The forest wants to kidnap me. The weeds at my feet are twining up my legs. They don't want me to leave. And the logical part of my brain knows the bird calls above are good sounds, but in my ears, they're screechy and eerie and terrible right now."

The trees, the weeds, the smells, the sounds—they weren't the real problem. But what was?

A thought flashed in her mind, and it grew, magnified, until it filled her.

"I feel alone here. Utterly alone." She backed out of the woods onto the lawn and hunched over.

Why did You leave me all alone, God? Why did You send me to Germany to be disappointed, abandoned, lost? I'm mad at You. Furious. And I know I shouldn't say that, because You're God, but I'm so angry.

Tears burned behind her eyes, and her lungs squeezed.

Why didn't You save me? Why did You let me go farther and farther into that forest? You could have guided me. You could have pointed me in the right direction. Why didn't You show me where to go?

Tears raced down her cheeks.

You left me. Mom left me. Dad left me.

Even Mimi left me.

Jade wiped her eyes and took deep breaths until she calmed down.

Bryan was leaving, too.

Maybe she was destined to be alone. She marched toward the gazebo. The twirly feelings that messed with her heartbeat when she was around Bryan needed taming.

She'd be smart to think of him as a friend. Only a friend.

Chapter Six

Bryan wanted more students, and he got them. As usual, the joke was on him.

"We didn't know you were teaching classes. Shelby and I would have signed up first thing. Tell me we haven't missed much." Beth Jones twirled her index finger around a lock of straight blond hair. Her skintight black pants looked more appropriate for an aerobics class, but Bryan didn't know much about fashion. If burrs got stuck in the skimpy material, that was her problem.

"Yeah, Bry, why you keeping it a secret?" Shelby Lattimer chewed a piece of gum and tightened her ponytail of long, wavy brown hair. She wore equally unsuitable pants, except hers were dark gray with a hot-pink stripe down the side of each leg.

Two years younger than Bryan, both Beth and Shelby had been flirting with him and his brothers since the ladies had turned thirteen. Beth had been engaged a few years ago, but Shelby rotated through the single guys in Lake Endwell. His sisters classified her as a serial dater. The way they said it made it sound similar to a serial killer. One thing he was sure of? Neither Beth nor Shelby had joined his class to learn about nature.

"The class isn't a secret." Bryan flexed his hands. "It's been on the town website for a month."

Why did *they* have to show up for his class? Why couldn't someone join who would actually get something out of it? Someone like Jade. Speaking of... Where was she?

"When did you get a dog?" Shelby's lips curled downward as she eyed Teeny.

"I'm taking care of her for a friend."

Beth touched his arm, gazing up at him through thick lashes and heavy eyeliner. "I can't wait to learn more about surviving in the great outdoors."

"Good." He shoved his sunglasses on top of his head. "We'll be heading out in a few minutes."

Voices from the parking lot diverted his attention. Jade strolled next to Sam. She tipped her head back and laughed at something he said.

Bryan ground his teeth together. This morning got better and better. When had they met? And why was it causing his blood to bubble at a low simmer?

"Hey." Sam waved to Bryan, but all his focus was on Jade. "I came to get Teeny, but maybe I should stay for the class."

"I'm watching Teeny." Jade grinned.

"Then I'll keep you company," Sam replied with an appreciative smile.

Bryan's temples tightened to the point of a blood clot. He searched Jade's face for a clue on what she was feeling, but he wasn't picking up on any discomfort at the idea of hanging out with his little brother. She'd crouched to pet behind Teeny's ears and was making baby talk to the smitten animal.

Sam grinned. "Hey, Beth. Shelby. Don't tell me you're interested in hiking." They greeted him as enthusiastically as they had Bryan, which Bryan took as a good sign. Maybe Sam *would* take the class. They'd flirt with Sam instead of him, and Bryan could concentrate on today's topic—building natural shelters. Not that any of them would pay attention, anyhow.

Jade straightened and smoothed her hair. He couldn't help but admire her outfit. Jeans, a long-sleeved plaid button-down over a tank top, and hiking boots. Much more appropriate than the other women's clothes.

Jade. All-American. All too appealing.

He looked at his hodgepodge class—not remotely the kinds of students he'd hoped to attract—and wished he'd never put those fliers up. But an image of the picturesque village near the retreat in Ontario came to mind. All week he'd spent hours clicking through websites of local attractions, including the nearby freshwater beaches, caves, hiking trails and cultural activities. He'd put up with the inevitable flirting for a chance to move there.

"Beth, Shelby," Bryan said. "I'd like you to meet Jade Emerson. She's opening a T-shirt shop in town."

"Oh, we heard about that." Beth and Shelby crowded around her. "Are you going to sell custom workout clothes?"

As Jade answered their questions, Bryan pulled Sam aside. "Are you really going to stay?"

Sam shrugged. "Might as well."

Bryan put a lid on his irritation. "Why don't you join the class?"

"No offense, brother, but don't you think Jade needs some help with Warhorse here?"

That kind of go-to attitude didn't come as a shock, but the sensation of swallowing a handful of thumbtacks hit Bryan, anyway. He wanted to be the one helping Jade with the dog, but what right did he have to interfere? None.

Bryan widened his stance. "Don't take her into the woods."

"Why not?"

He wasn't spilling Jade's secrets. Secrets weren't shared lightly. "Teeny might see a rabbit or something, and we both know how that would go."

"Don't worry. I'll be right there if Teeny gets out of line."

That's what Bryan worried about. Jade did not need his brother gawking over her. Now how was he going to focus on teaching? He glanced at Beth and Shelby. He should drop them off at a juice bar where they belonged. Sam had resumed his spot next to Jade.

He'd better get this over with. "Let's go."

Jade held Teeny's leash and tried to drag her eyes from Bryan. His thin grayish-blue shirt, jeans and hiking boots suited him, and his stubble made him appear more rugged, more attractive, more everything.

The two bombshells fawning over him? Both were friendly. Maybe a tad too flirty with the Sheffield brothers, but who could blame them? The Sheffield men had been blessed with good looks and winning personalities. From the hearsay Jade gathered each morning at the Daily Donut, the Sheffields were considered Lake Endwell's first family.

Bryan strode away with Beth and Shelby chatting on either side of him. What would it feel like to be part of a respected, close-knit family? Both her parents were certainly respected, but she'd been excluded from the mix. Although they were blood related, she'd always been an outsider with her nose pressed to the window of their lives. Would she have turned out differently if one of her brilliant parents had raised her?

She hitched her chin. Who cared? She'd turned out fine with Mimi's help.

The blonde and brunette flanked Bryan, leaning in and laughing as they headed across a small lawn. Jade glanced down at her plaid red shirt over a white tank top. Definitely hillbilly compared to the sporty, body-shaping outfits Beth and Shelby wore.

"Today we're making natural shelters." Bryan's voice carried.

"Do you want me to take her?" Sam held his hand out.

With a start, Jade jerked her chin toward him. "What?"

"Teeny. Want me to take her?"

She attempted to smile. "No, I've got it." Sam resembled Bryan, but he had a less serious air about him. They shared those brilliant blue eyes, an athletic build and dark blond hair, although Sam's was more brown than Bryan's.

"I'm surprised she's this calm." Sam matched Jade's stride. "She almost pulled me off my feet earlier when she saw a leaf blow across the yard."

"You should have seen her at obedience class. She chased down a Chihuahua. The poor pup cowered under a chair. It wasn't pretty."

Sam chuckled. "Do you have a dog? You're good with her."

"No, but animals like me. I have no idea why."

"Probably because you have an easy way about you," Sam said. "I ran into Libby the other day and she went on and on about your store. You'd think she was the one opening it."

"Really?" Jade took it as a compliment. "When she and your aunt Sally stopped by, the space was empty. I've set the display tables up now. No merchandise yet, but I'm working on it. So where are we taking little Miss Teeny?"

"The path Bryan is on leads to a big clearing. It has a nice view."

"Do we have to walk through trees?" She nibbled her fingernail.

Sam looked taken aback, but he thought about it. "Maybe twenty feet. The path is paved and wide. We'll be able to handle Teeny."

Twenty feet. To a clearing with a view. Could she do it? "I don't know."

"It's my favorite spot out here."

She didn't want to tell him about her fear. Maybe she'd be okay.

Or maybe she needed to be honest with Sam. Stay where it was safe.

Sam chattered about a movie, and she took a deep breath, trying to keep her mind on what he was saying.

"After the movie, Libby told me about your T-shirts. Said something about jewelry, too. She kept gabbing on about Moira and her custom necklaces."

"Libby mentioned Moira, but I haven't contacted her yet." Jade hadn't contacted Libby, either. She'd wanted to text Libby several times, but she felt funny about it. Would Libby think she was glomming on to her?

Memories of lonely months in New York City kicked around in her mind. Making new friends had been stressful. One of the women at work initially seemed eager to spend time with her, but when Jade called to make plans, the woman evaded her. It was so embarrassing. Since then, Jade had a hard time deciphering whether someone genuinely wanted to get to know her or was just saying the right thing to be nice.

"Don't worry. When Libby has something in her head, she doesn't rest until it's done. She'll be knocking on your door any day now. Guaranteed. But don't feel pressured into it."

Jade hoped he was right. She liked Libby. And she wanted friends.

They reached the path, and as if on cue, her throat tightened and vision blurred. Jade wound Teeny's leash around her hand twice to shorten it. Her heartbeat thumped in her chest.

Go time.

But could she go? In there?

Sam turned to her and frowned. "You coming?"

"I, um…" She blinked rapidly, her stomach heaving. Teeny caught sight of something and dashed forward, jolting Jade off her feet. Her legs steamrolled ahead, and she had to fight to keep her balance.

"Hey, stop!" Sam called to Teeny, but the dog ignored him. "Teeny, stop!"

Jade yanked the leash, forced her body to freeze and hoped she wouldn't hyperventilate.

A few seconds later, Bryan appeared, his cheekbones etched against his skin. He took the leash from Jade, handed it to Sam and jerked his chin back the way he'd come. "Beth and Shelby are in the clearing. Go with them a minute, will you, Sam? Have them start gathering leaves and twigs."

Sam opened his mouth to reply but must have thought better of it. He jogged with Teeny up the path.

Jade's pulse pounded in her ears. Bryan put his hand on her shoulder. She almost leaned into it. Safe. Protective. "I'm sorry, Jade."

"Why? I'm fine." She fanned herself. She was not in danger. The dog barely dragged her.

"No, you're not. The dumb dog." The muscle in his cheek flickered.

"It's not her fault. I should have paid better attention."
She wrapped her arms around her waist, her fingertips
digging into her skin. What had she expected? She'd embarrassed herself. Why couldn't she be normal? Why did
this have to be so hard?

"I'm sorry. I can't. I just…" She shook her head and
jogged backward, not taking her eyes off Bryan.

"Jade, wait," Bryan called. Jade wended in the direction of the parking lot. When he caught up to her, he took
her by the arm. A hundred things to say jumbled in his
head, but the only thing that came out was, "I'm sorry."

"I already told you it's my fault." She wouldn't meet
his eyes. "I thought I might be okay. I should have known
better."

"Teeny's a nuisance."

"You can't blame the dog. I feel stupid, so I'm going
home." After pulling her keys from her pocket, she
pressed the unlock button. *Chirp. Chirp.*

Bryan blocked her by flattening his hand against the
car door. He stood inches from her, all too aware of her
vulnerability. He wanted to hold her, soothe her, make
it all better.

"Wait." His stomach plummeted at the hollowness in
her eyes. Something more was there than fear. Something deeper.

She shook her head. "You need to get back to Beth
and Shelby."

"I'm where I need to be. Neither of them care about
building natural shelters, anyhow."

"How can you say that?" A flush rose to her cheeks.
"They showed up today, didn't they? Now go back there
so you can write down the hours or whatever you're supposed to log."

"Not until I'm sure you're okay," he said, keeping his voice low.

"I'm fine."

He pressed closer, taking her hand. He was skating on the thinnest sheet of ice. Five years he'd denied himself. Attraction, affection—all off-limits. What would happen when the ice shattered? If he opened his heart a crack, he'd get hurt. Women didn't want the quiet life he enjoyed. They wanted someone dynamic. Someone the exact opposite of him.

Didn't matter. He wasn't going to date Jade. He didn't want to date anyone. But God had crossed their paths for a reason.

"Remember the day we met, what Libby said over pizza?" Bryan asked.

"I remember."

"Do you believe God planned this?"

"Yes." She rubbed her arm. "Mimi always told me everything happens for a reason. When I go to church, I hear the same message."

"I think He leads us all the time."

"Yeah, me, too."

"But it doesn't mean I always listen to Him."

Her face blanked, then her eyebrows drew together. "Do you hear Him?"

"I haven't heard an audible voice or seen a burning bush." He raked his fingers through his hair. He rarely discussed religion with anyone. He showed up to church, prayed, read the Bible and that was it. The words flamed to life, though. "But I know when I'm being spiritually prompted."

"I do, too."

"Libby verbalized what I've been feeling since the day we met—God introduced us for a reason."

Her eyes darted back and forth. He was making a mess of this. He'd never been good at heart-to-hearts. Now she probably thought he was losing his mind.

"I think God wants you here in Lake Endwell," he said. "And I think I'm supposed to help you."

"I agree with you about Lake Endwell, but…" She avoided his eyes and shrugged. "You don't have to help me."

"I want to help." He bent slightly to look into her eyes. *No one ever needs me. But you do.* She hesitated and smiled. It reached in and plucked a string loose from his heart, unraveling the ragged patch job he'd slapped together when Abby walked out.

Jade stood on her tiptoes, wrapped her arms around his neck and gave him a hug. "Thanks."

And Bryan forgot how to breathe. "I'd better get back to class."

Chapter Seven

"Where are we going?" Jade asked the next afternoon.

Bryan kept one hand on the steering wheel as he adjusted the volume. An upbeat country song played. "You'll see."

"That's reassuring." Faint freckles smattered her nose, and her face angled upward to catch the sunlight through the truck window.

He'd been up front with Jade about his Canada plans, but was he misleading her by spending all this time together? She had to have guessed he found her attractive. Did she know he anticipated their Wednesdays and Sundays a little too much? While he was committed to helping her, he had to do a better job at keeping it casual.

Maybe he was overthinking the whole thing.

Granddad's stately cabin came into view. The blue lake glistened behind it. He pulled his truck into the drive and cut the engine. "This was my grandfather's cottage."

"Wow! It's amazing." She jumped out of the truck, shutting the door behind her. He met her at the end of the driveway where two sets of stairs began. One led to the deck, the other to the kitchen door. Almost May, they'd been blessed with a heavy dose of sunshine, no wind and sixty-degree temperatures.

"Come on. I'll show you around." He unlocked the kitchen door and ushered her inside.

"It's even prettier in here, and I didn't think that was possible. Look at the view. Incredible." She scurried to the wall of windows showcasing the deck, the lawn and the dock. "Does anyone live here?"

"No, we use it for family gatherings. Out-of-town guests stay once in a while. It's part of the family." He loved this place. Polished wood floors, vaulted ceilings, open floor plan. "I'll give you the tour, and we can go outside."

She oohed and aahed through each room, but he kept it short and slid open the patio door. Jade bypassed the outdoor furniture and stood at the rail, her arms resting on the edge. He took the spot next to her.

"I'm speechless." She beamed at him. "It's stunning."

"I thought you'd like it."

"I do."

Robins swooped from branches above to the yard below, and a kayaker paddled near the shore. The quiet shush of a breeze added to the solitude.

"Want to go down to the dock?" He gestured to the lake, and her serene smile made his mouth almost drop open. "This way. My sister Claire and her husband, Reed, live in the yellow cottage."

"It's adorable," Jade said. "And right next door."

"I'll introduce you sometime. You'll like Claire. Everyone does."

He took out two chairs from the storage shed and set them up at the end of the dock. Jade sat in one, and he lowered his body into the other. A fish jumped several feet away, causing a splash.

"Did you see that?" Jade pointed at the ripples. "A fish just jumped!"

"You'll see a lot of them." He studied her profile. The slight slope of her nose, the high cheekbones, lashes curling up. Everything about her right now seemed like a kid opening a birthday present. "You like the water, don't you?"

She nodded. "Yes. I actually feel relaxed, and I can't stop admiring all those shimmers."

"Have you ever been on a boat?"

"No." She shook her head. "I haven't."

"We have a fishing boat, canoes, kayaks and a pontoon."

She snuggled into the chair. "I like it right here."

"So do I. See over there?" He stretched his arm to the left. "That tree line?"

She craned her neck. "Cedars, pines and other evergreens?"

"You've been studying." He nodded. "About three miles west of them, if you drive on old Ranger Road, there's a field with a broken fence. Granddad would take me there. We'd hike about a mile north through the farm field into a forest. A trickle of a river runs through the woods, and beyond is a large meadow surrounded by great towering trees."

She watched him, and at her rapt attention, he quickly looked away.

"Granddad told me he always went there when he needed clarity. He said it's where he felt closest to God. If he was unsure of something, he would camp a night or two until he knew what to do."

"No offense to your grandfather or anything, but close to God or not, I'm not camping in the middle of a bunch of trees. Ever."

"Never?" he teased. Then he grew serious. "It didn't work for me, anyhow."

"So you tried it? The camping thing?"

"I've camped too many times to count, but yeah, when Abby moved out, I hiked to his spot, camped for three days."

He hadn't planned on mentioning Abby.

"And?" She lowered her chin and stared up at him through those green eyes.

"And I let her go. Signed the divorce papers."

"Why?" she asked quietly.

"She cheated on me." His heart clenched at the admission. It was still hard to reconcile. The woman he vowed to love and cherish had loved and cherished someone else while married to him. "I'm not proud of this, but a part of me was relieved when she left."

"Cheated on you?" Her nose scrunched as her eyebrows dipped.

"Yeah, she moved to Texas not long after. Got married a few weeks following our divorce." The familiar ache in his chest didn't burn as much as it normally did when he thought about that time. "I'll be honest, all we did was fight. I was a bad husband and she wasn't a great wife."

She touched his arm. "This isn't something you talk about much, do you?"

"No. I never thought I'd be the type of guy to get a divorce. I believe in vows, commitment, forever."

"So do I."

Something in those three words clanged warnings in his brain. He treaded on dangerous territory. "That's why I'm never getting married again. And I'm not interested in dating, either."

Jade fought to keep her face from crumpling. It wasn't as if she didn't know it—they had no future together—

but hearing it come out of his mouth slapped her to reality.

"I hope you didn't think I'm interested in that way." She plastered on a tight smile. "Dating you never crossed my mind."

His face slackened, and she felt a little bad, but not enough to take it back. Did he think every girl wanted to date him? Well, they probably did. He was just too—she glanced at him—wonderful. Handsome, honest, generous. The exact type of guy she'd been hoping to find all these years.

Bryan gave her a sheepish look. "I didn't mean it the way it came out."

"No?" Still sitting, she leaned to peer over the edge of the dock. Could this conversation be any more awkward?

"I just wanted you to know…"

"I appreciate you confiding in me. People get divorced, Bryan. Then they find someone else, and they try again."

"Not me." Bryan clasped his hands lightly in his lap.

"Why not?" She shouldn't be prying, but curiosity won. He was young, successful and a genuinely good person. Didn't he deserve to be happy?

"I'm not going through that again."

"Not every woman cheats."

The muscle in his cheek pulsed. "It's more than that."

"I'm not following you."

"I married Abby for the wrong reasons."

She shifted to face him. "Like what?"

"Marriage is about love and commitment. I mean, I loved her, but really, I was following what I thought was the script for my life." He shook his head. "My brother Tommy got engaged a few months before me. I always did everything he did. And Abby had been hinting about a ring."

"How long did you two date?"

His lips drew together. "Not long enough. I didn't understand her."

"Do any of us understand each other?"

"I don't know. But if I had worked harder to understand Abby before we got married, I would have realized she and I weren't meant to be. I had plenty of warning signs. I ignored my instincts. Prayer wasn't a big part of my life back then."

Jade thought about it a minute. The truth of his words churned her stomach. He'd been hurt. She had no right to ask him all these personal questions, and the more she learned, the more she sympathized with him. However, if he was astute enough to know he wouldn't have married Abby if he understood her, then he was smart enough to figure it out with Jade. Her dating life had always been about inverse proportions. The longer she dated a guy, the less he liked her.

Everyone she ever loved left her, usually sooner rather than later. Mimi was the one exception. Even if Bryan wasn't moving and somehow developed romantic feelings for Jade, it would only be a matter of time before he'd bail, too.

"I'm sorry your marriage hurt you so deeply. Since you're being honest with me, I'll be truthful with you. When men really get to know me, they realize we weren't meant to be, either."

"What aren't you telling me?" He met her gaze.

"Nothing." She lifted one shoulder. "I'm glad we're friends without the extra baggage. My store and getting over this fear are my top priorities."

"Those men you dated," he said gruffly. "They weren't worth your time."

"I agree. A boyfriend isn't on my agenda right now,

anyway. I'm going to be very selective when I do date." And in fantasyland, Bryan Sheffield would be her first choice.

Two ducks flew in front of them, landing feetfirst in the lake with water spraying behind them. She'd never seen ducks enter the water before. Messy. Kind of like her move here. But they paddled calmly as if the loud entry never happened.

"Have you ever gotten serious with anyone?" Bryan leaned back, propping his ankle on the opposite knee.

"Not to the point of getting engaged." She shielded her eyes from the sun. "The guys I've dated had strong opinions about my life choices."

"What was wrong with your choices?"

"Everything." Jade let out a hollow laugh. "Let's see, one told me I worked too many hours. Another told me I wasn't working hard enough if I wanted a promotion— mind you, I didn't want a promotion. The complaints were always silly. My clothes were too casual. My hair too messy. And you'd think I hid dead bodies in my base-ment the way my last boyfriend flipped out when I told him I was quitting my job and moving back to Las Vegas to take care of Mimi." Her mood lifted as she admitted all this. She flashed a smile to Bryan. "It took me almost two years to realize I'd been dating the same type of guy, and I will never be able to please that type."

"They were stupid. You shouldn't change a thing. You're…well, you're something, Jade."

Her throat tightened. "I like who I am, Bryan, but I'm not *something*. I'm never going to cure cancer or be a top ranked surgeon or raise millions of dollars for homeless children. I'm opening a little T-shirt shop in a small town. That's it."

"You don't have to cure cancer to be special."

Her breath caught as his words seeped in. Pressure built behind her eyes, and she lurched to her feet. "Sure."

He rose, grabbing her arm before she could escape. "Why do you do that? Act like you're not important?"

"I don't know what you're talking about." She stilled as his hand caressed her arm.

"I think you do." He touched her hair. His eyes changed to the exact shade of the sky above them. He leaned in. "I don't like it."

"You don't have to like it. This is me. It's what you get."

"Yeah, and what you've got is pretty good."

Emotion clogged her throat. She couldn't do this. Couldn't argue with him.

He pulled his hand away. "I'll drop it, Jade. For now."

Good, because if he said another nice thing to her, she would burst into tears and who knew what would happen then. Her heart was already in way too deep. If she started to believe him, she would sink. And he wouldn't be around to prevent her from drowning.

What kind of moron would let a jewel like Jade slip through his fingers? Bryan flexed his hand as he thought about the men Jade dated. He wanted to find their names and hunt them down. Show them what he thought about their mind games.

Bryan followed Tommy to his living room and sat on the massive sectional later that night to watch baseball. His thoughts tumbled around in his mind. Maybe Tommy would help him untangle them. But Bryan would have to confide about the job in Blue Mountain first. It was time.

"How's the class going?" Tommy handed Bryan an ice cold can of soda before joining him on the couch.

Moisture dripped down the side of the can as he

cracked it open and took a drink. "It's a joke. Guess who showed up yesterday?"

Tommy raised his eyebrows and shrugged.

"Beth, Shelby and our dear brother, Sam."

Tommy choked on his drink and coughed a few times, pounding his chest with his fist. "Why would those three ever want to take a class on outdoor survival?"

Bryan shrugged. "Got me. The ladies showed up in skimpy workout gear like they were ready for aerobics or yoga or whatever they do. Sam didn't actually come for the class. He helped Jade with Teeny until she had to leave."

"Jade?" He clicked through channels with the remote until he found the game. "Is this the girl who Libby was talking about?"

"She's opening a T-shirt shop in the old record store."

"Ah, the old record store. Remember when we would go in there and buy CDs after we got our allowance? Aunt Sally must have bought every Beach Boys album. Wasn't it a vacuum repair shop for a while?"

"Yeah, and after that an insurance agency."

Tommy nodded. "I'm glad another business is going in there."

"Me, too," Bryan said. "Next time Sheffield Auto needs plaques, decals or shirts, we should order them from her. She does custom designs."

"Is something more going on? You're holding out on me, aren't you?"

Bryan was, but not in the way Tommy implied. "She's helping me take Teeny to obedience class, and I'm teaching her on Sunday afternoons."

His eyes twinkled as he grinned over his Coke.

"She's all alone here with no one to look out for her." Bryan shrugged. "You would do the same."

A cocky smile spread across Tommy's face. "You do that, Bry. Keep looking out for her."

"It's not like that."

"Like what?" His tone was pure innocence. "You're giving her private lessons. She's helping with the dog. Sounds friendly to me."

"Yeah, well, it is friendly. Just friends." Bryan set his drink on the end table. "I need to tell you something. I'm teaching the survival class and giving Jade private lessons because I applied to be an outdoor leader at a corporate retreat. It's in Blue Mountain, Ontario."

His expression clouded. "But Ontario is in Canada."

Bryan nodded.

"It's a temporary job, right?"

Bryan shook his head.

Tommy sprung to his feet and began pacing. "What about…?" He pivoted and waved his finger at Bryan. "Why?"

He didn't answer.

"You'd turn your back on Sheffield Auto? Who will run your dealerships?"

"If you and Sam don't want to split mine and each take one, Dawson could run them. He's been with me four years. He knows what he's doing."

"He's not a Sheffield." Tommy glared at Bryan. "Why are you doing this?"

Tempted to stand, Bryan stayed put and tapped his fingertips against his thigh. "I can't keep on like this."

"Like what?"

He glanced around the room and saw baby dolls and plastic play food in a pink bin. Kleenex boxes and candles. A vase of tulips. All evidence Tom had a full life, complete with wife and kids.

"I'm never going to have this." Bryan stood, gesturing to the room. "It's too hard to stay. I'm glad you're married, and I'm happy you're having another baby. I'm glad Claire found Reed, and Libby and Jake are living the dream. But I'm not getting married again. I'll never have a family of my own."

He narrowed his eyes. "There's no law against you finding a wife."

Maybe not, but he didn't know how to explain. Bryan rounded the couch to the bank of windows overlooking the backyard carpeted with velvety green grass. "No."

"Why not?" Tommy followed him and leaned against the window.

"I have my reasons."

"They aren't all like Abby, Bryan."

"It was humiliating. Sometimes I'm more mad about that than the rest—she stole my trust."

Tommy put his hand on Bryan's shoulder. "I know. I've been there. But I think you do trust people. Maybe you're scared to trust a woman completely, but if you pray on it, God will help you."

Bryan shook his head. "I've made peace with my decision." Well, he had until Jade moved to town. Their dockside chat this afternoon left his thoughts in a war zone. "If I get the job, I'm moving. I could be content up there."

"And you can't here?"

Bryan didn't respond.

"I take it no one else knows."

"No," Bryan said. "And I want to keep it that way."

"When will you find out about the job?"

"They're interviewing people in June. If I get it, I need to be there in July." Bryan filled him in on where the Blue Mountains were located and the types of skills he needed to show the director. "I wouldn't be in charge of rock climbing or anything like that. They have a local instructor. I would be their survival and hiking guide. That's why I offered the class here. But the way it's going, I won't have the requirements, anyhow."

"What are you talking about? You already have the requirements for the job."

"Not as an instructor. They want logs. I'd have to demonstrate my qualifications."

"Don't worry about it. You're a natural. It's hiking, not curing cancer."

Bryan frowned. What had Jade said earlier? That she wasn't *something*. She wasn't finding a cure for cancer, just opening a little store and she was fine with it.

Maybe he did understand how Jade felt. Maybe it hit a little too close to home. Maybe after Abby left he'd convinced himself he wasn't *something*, either.

"So you aren't dating Jade?" Tommy asked. "Does she know you're only giving her lessons to beef up your résumé?"

"She knows." Bryan flexed his hand. "We had a long talk this afternoon. I believe she used the phrase 'Dating you has never crossed my mind.'"

Tommy snorted. "Well, that leaves things less complicated."

Hardly. The more Bryan replayed Jade's declaration they were meant to be friends, the less friend-like his feelings veered. When they'd stood on the dock earlier, he'd wanted to hold her. Kiss her.

What kind of guy was he? He no sooner told her he'd never marry again, and instantly he wanted to kiss her? That's why he couldn't trust himself. He made bad decisions when it came to women. He'd be better off in Canada. He'd find himself a private cabin in the woods. The single life was for him.

Chapter Eight

"You bring up a good point, Libby." Jade tapped her chin Monday afternoon and surveyed the mess in front of her. Boxes were stacked along the perimeter of the store, and the tables she'd assembled were empty. "A revolving jewelry display would fit nicely here, and it wouldn't take up much room."

"I'll be back in a few hours with Moira." Libby hiked her purse strap over her shoulder and waved goodbye. "You're going to flip over her necklaces."

"Thanks again." Jade walked her to the door, admiring the new sign she'd installed this morning. She'd painted the large wooden circle creamy beige, and deep purple letters spelled out Shine Gifts, matching the accent wall behind the counter. She couldn't wait to create the window display, but first things first, it was time to play with her new equipment and make some T-shirt samples. She practically sprinted to the back room.

For a moment she stood in the doorway and took it all in. It smelled like plastic and ink and fresh paint. She'd purchased the machines on credit. It would take a few years to pay them off, but it would be worth it. A large worktable filled the center of the room. Her heat presses were ready to go on the counter against the wall. She'd bought a commercial sprayer to pretreat material, and she'd stashed the other accessories—rhinestones, decals, engraving stock, hot fix transfer tape—in the cabinets above and below the counter.

Jade strolled around the room, her fingers trailing lovingly on each and every tool. This was hers. All hers.

Her cell phone rang. Her first instinct was to ignore it, but what if it was Bryan?

She'd been trying to get Sunday's conversation off her mind, but his comment about not having to cure cancer to be special kept pinching her heart. If she didn't try harder to protect her emotions, she'd be devastated. It wasn't as if she hadn't been down this dreamy-eyed road before. First with her parents, then with the guys she dated.

If she worked at it, she could prevent a heartbreak. Bryan wasn't into dating, either, so that helped a lot. Another month or so and most likely he'd be gone. The phone rang again. She hesitated before checking the ID.

Mom.

She raised her eyes to the ceiling. She didn't talk to her mother much due to the time difference and her mom's busy schedule. In fact, they'd only spoken once since Jade moved to Lake Endwell. She'd better answer this.

"Hi, Mom."

"Jade." Her name stretched like thick caramel. "I have good news. Priscilla told Gerald the woman they hired at the advertising firm in Paris already quit. I'm booking your flight. What city is best for you to fly out of—Detroit or Chicago?"

"Neither." Jade swiped a package of white tees from the cupboard. "I'm all set to open my store here."

A long pause with faint crackling ensued. "But Paris…"

"I know. Paris is incredible, and you and Gerald are looking out for me, but I have to try this."

"I thought you'd be thrilled at the chance to work in Paris."

Jade counted to three. Maybe her mother had the right to feel that way. Maybe Jade hadn't been clear enough about how important opening this business was to her.

"I appreciate it, Mom, I really do. But all my equipment arrived, and I'm getting ready to try out some of my designs. You should see them. I'm making rhinestone shirts, oh, and I have this great idea for tote bags…"

"Rhinestones and tote bags." She didn't sound pleased. "I'll tell Priscilla to hold the thought and let us know if anything else comes up."

Jade stretched her neck from side to side to relieve some of the tension gripping it. "I don't think it will be necessary. I'm staying here."

"For now." The words were clipped.

"Forever."

"Forever is a long time. You'll get bored. Making T-shirts isn't going to fulfill you. You want to be respected."

Jade decided to ignore half the speech. "If I get bored, I'll visit you in France."

They chatted a few more minutes before ending the conversation. Jade tossed the phone onto the counter and cracked her knuckles. Would she get bored of making T-shirts? And why did Mom think she wouldn't be respected? Owning a business was respectable.

Well, owning a *successful* business was. What if no one came in to buy her shirts? What if months went by with paltry sales and she ran through her money and had to close it down?

She still wouldn't move to Paris.

Jade pulled a stool over, propped her elbows on the worktable and let her chin drop on her fists. What was there in Paris for her, anyhow? Her mother simply wanted Jade in a glamorous city doing respected work, whatever that was. But Jade had given up trying to earn either of her parents' approval.

They didn't understand her, and they probably never would.

She unfolded a shirt and spread it onto the printing machine. She had things to do. Shirts to make. She tucked the excess material under the platens, selected the design she'd created yesterday and tried to remember which button to push.

Her first guess was correct and soon the printer was swiping back and forth, leaving her free with her thoughts again.

Thoughts of Mom. The lingering effects of being ignored by both parents. Jade sniffed. All those little-girl fantasies swirled back.

The fantasies stopped after her summer in Germany. Mimi had talked Mom into letting seven-year-old Jade spend summer vacation with her. Gerald had accepted a temporary grant program in Spain, so it was only Jade and her mom. The days leading up to the trip were filled with ideas of playing dolls, having tea parties and being best friends with Mom. In the crevices of her heart, she believed her mother would see how good she was and ask Jade to live with her.

It took three days for reality to set in. Her mother's long hours at the research center and unreliable baby-sitters left Jade alone too often. The rental house was old, made of stones, like something out of a fairy tale. It nestled up against a thick forest.

No.

Jade slapped the table. She was over it. It wasn't a big deal.

She was twenty-seven. A big girl. And if she moved to Paris, she would be devastated again, because she'd want a real relationship with her mother, and Mom wanted to cure cancer.

Curing cancer. How could anyone compete with that?

Jade blew out a breath and checked on the printer. The bright colors chased some of the resentment away. Opening her laptop, she clicked through to the design software. Her double major in advertising and graphic design wouldn't go to waste, regardless of what her mother thought.

Which reminded her, she needed to work on a website. Online sales were vital in today's economy. Maybe she could set up an Etsy shop, too. She would go door-to-door if she had to, but Jade would make a life for herself in Lake Endwell. No matter what.

"Come in. I'll just be a minute."

Bryan stepped into the hallway of Jade's apartment and shut the door behind him. He was ten minutes early, but he didn't want to be late for Teeny's obedience class.

"Have a seat in the living room," Jade called from what he presumed was her bedroom. He cautiously treaded through the tidy kitchen past a dining table into the living room. Beige walls. Tan carpeting. Big navy couch with furry gray pillows.

He smiled, shaking his head. The pillows made sense since this was Jade's place. He poked around, bending to inspect the framed photos on the tables and walls. Almost every picture was of Jade laughing, her arms around a white-haired woman with kind eyes. Mimi, if he had to guess. Two well-dressed couples were displayed in a side-by-side frame on the far end table.

He crossed to the front of the room where two windows overlooked the road. A one-story building held a hair salon directly across the street, and a four-square brick house stood next to it.

Jade had no window coverings. Anyone could see in. Bryan didn't like the idea of someone watching her.

"Hey, Jade, did you ever buy those curtains?" He eye-balled the window casings. Thirty-two-inch rods would probably work if he drilled into the wall above the trim.

She entered the room with her hair waving past her shoulders and wearing a black-and-gray-striped shirt scooped at the neck. She adjusted her sleeves. "What?"

"You look pretty." He closed his eyes and almost groaned. He wasn't a blurter, so why had those words come out of his mouth?

Because they're true. She was beautiful. The way her cheeks flushed and eyes sparkled, he guessed she liked the compliment.

"Thanks," she said softly.

He cleared his throat. "Did you buy curtains?"

"Yeah, they're still in the package, though. I haven't had a chance to iron them or anything." She disappeared into the kitchen and came back with her purse. "Do you have the clicker? The treats?"

"Yes." Tearing his gaze from her, he checked his watch. "After class, I'll drop Teeny off at home and grab my drill. I'll hang the curtains tonight."

She waved in dismissal. "Oh, don't worry about that. I can do it."

"I am worried about it. It's been over two weeks." He widened his stance, crossing his arms over his chest. "I don't want people staring in at you."

She scrunched her nose. "No one is watching me."

"How do you know that? People come and go all the time to the hair place, and I think the brick house across the street is rented out to some college punks." Now that he thought about it, her locks were on the flimsy side. "We'll stop at the hardware store and get a dead bolt, too. No sense messing around with your safety."

"College kids don't live there. It's an old woman. Margaret. She sits on her porch when it's nice out. Her husband died a few years ago."

Margaret Nettles. He'd forgotten about her, and he'd lived here his whole life. Shame on him. "Well, you still need curtains and a strong lock."

"Okay, fine, I'll put them up. Now, let's get going. We don't want to be late."

Her words should have pacified him, but they didn't. Jade didn't have anyone to look out for her. No family or friends in town to rely on. And he shouldn't be taking on this role, but the role was there and no one seemed to be filling it. He couldn't in good conscience leave tonight without doing the bare minimum to protect her.

"It's not fine." He stepped toward her, close enough to smell her flowery shampoo. It hit him again how petite she was, how vulnerable. "I'm installing them tonight."

"But, Bryan, I…"

"Why are you arguing about this?"

She set her shoulders, tilting her chin up. "Why are you so insistent?"

The challenge shooting from her posture lit his pulse. "I worry about you here. Alone."

"I'm not helpless." Her lashes lowered a fraction.

"I didn't say you were." He softened his tone. "I… Just let me do this."

He waited for her to ask why, but he wouldn't know

how to explain. The thought of something happening to her, someone hurting her—he couldn't let that happen.

"Okay, but I don't want you to feel obligated. I'm sure I can rig them up somehow."

He hadn't realized he was holding his breath until it escaped. "I don't feel obligated."

I feel responsible. Protective.

She smiled and tilted her head to the door.

He had the most curious urge to tell her she could rely on him. For curtains, for locks, for anything.

Instead, he followed her outside.

He'd picked a funny time in life to grow feelings for a woman. And not any woman. This one. This independent, courageous, off-limits woman was wreaking havoc with his plans.

Sunday morning Jade slipped into the back pew of church. Libby had given her the address and service times when she brought Moira around with the jewelry. Libby was right—Moira's jewelry was stunning—and Jade figured, why not?

But try a new church? Jade hadn't been praying like she normally did, because guilt had crept in over freaking out that day in City Park. Who was she to be mad at God? She was surprised He hadn't shot lightning bolts at her. She bowed her head.

Lord, I'm sorry. And I'm not just saying that so You don't punish me. I shouldn't have blamed You. I know all about free will, but I still don't like it. I don't like that little girls can be neglected or lost.

For a moment, she had the feeling God agreed. He didn't like little girls to be neglected or lost, either.

Jade leafed through the bulletin. She missed her worship home in Las Vegas. Some called it a megachurch since it used to be a movie theater complex, but to her it was Sunday mornings with God's word. This, on the other hand, could never be described as a megachurch. Postcard perfect, the outside boasted white siding, a towering steeple and tall, narrow stained-glass windows depicting Bible scenes. Inside, the arched entryway led to a wide aisle with burgundy carpet and rows of pews on both sides. Organ music filled the air. The faint smell of lemon, most likely a wood cleaner, and smoke from the matches used to light the candles added to the atmosphere.

She didn't recognize any of the hymns listed in the program. Old-fashioned. The church she attended as a child with Mimi always played hymns like "Rock of Ages," and she remembered the organ player having a robust style. But Mimi's church congregation had grown smaller over the years and the donations dwindled, forcing the church to close.

This church was pretty full. Not likely to have the same problems as Mimi's.

Jade hoped she'd be able to follow along.

More people streamed inside, and her breath caught when Bryan entered. His eyes met hers, and he smiled. She smiled back, her heartbeat fluttering like ribbons in the wind.

She waited for him to continue down the aisle. Libby and Jake sat next to Bryan's dad near the front. The other couple next to them? Likely another set of siblings. Bryan seemed to have an infinite supply. But he shuffled sideways through the pew and sat next to her.

Oh, boy.

His faint yet musky cologne put her on high alert. She was hyperaware of his dark dress pants inches from her swirly skirt. He wore a white-and-gray-pinstriped shirt with a burgundy tie. His short dark blond hair had been tamed with hair gel, and he'd shaved.

Have mercy. Was she having heart palpitations?

"Hey," he whispered, "hope you don't mind if I sit here."

Mind? Nope. She didn't mind. He could sit his gorgeous frame right there every Sunday.

"Are the curtains thick enough? You haven't had any trouble with the lock, have you?"

"Everything is great," she said quietly. "Thanks again."

After Wednesday night's interesting obedience class, where they were supposed to teach Teeny to lie down but failed miserably, Bryan, true to his word, had put up her curtains. Since it was faster to press the curtains with her machines downstairs, she'd given him a tour of her workshop. He'd asked a lot of questions and seemed impressed by the work she'd done.

She liked him. A little too much. Maybe he shouldn't sit his gorgeous frame anywhere near her. For her safety.

The pastor appeared up front and opened the service. Jade selected a hymnal and tried to find the song, paging through until she landed on the right spot. The congregation joined in singing "When I Survey the Wondrous Cross." Jade sang softly, and Bryan's voice melded with hers. As the service continued, she relaxed.

The pastor read from the Bible about a woman who had been subject to bleeding for twelve years. "This woman believed by simply touching Jesus' cloak, she would be healed. And Jesus affirmed her faith by healing her. It's important to remember the power of faith. Twelve years this woman suffered, but she believed God could heal her, and He did."

Jade gripped her hands together. Twelve years was a

long time. Jade probably would have resigned herself to a lifetime of suffering.

"Whatever you struggle with—sickness, financial problems, worry, fear—trust in God's mercy. Keep praying. Give your struggles to God every day. Be persistent. He loves you. He might not take away your problems, but He promises to give you peace."

She dipped her chin, frowning. She hadn't prayed about her fear in years. The congregation rose. Jade sprang to her feet.

"May the peace of God, which transcends all understanding, keep your hearts and your minds in Christ Jesus."

"Amen," everyone said.

The rest of the service passed, but Jade kept coming back to the pastor's advice about persisting in prayer. She wanted to try.

The final hymn played, and ushers directed people out. Bryan waited for her to exit the pew, then followed her down the aisle. The hum of quiet conversation enveloped Jade, and she inhaled the peace of the sanctuary until stopping to shake the pastor's hand. He welcomed her, urging her to come back anytime.

Bryan directed her away from the stream of people.

"Jade! You made it. I didn't see you earlier." Libby's long blond hair was pulled back in a low ponytail, and she wore stylish black pants with a fuchsia jacket that nipped at the waist and flared out with a ruffle. "Come on, we're all going to Pat's Diner for breakfast."

Jade weighed her options. On one hand, she'd been spending entirely too much time with Bryan, but on the other hand, Bryan and his family made her feel welcome, comfortable.

She glanced at him but couldn't discern much. He

wasn't chiming in to urge her to join them or anything, which was good. It reminded her he was helping her because he was nice and wanted a job a million miles away, not because he had feelings for her.

"Thanks," Jade said. "Maybe another time."

She'd follow his lead. Keep their interactions limited to the outdoor sessions and dog obedience classes, and in the meantime she'd think of all the reasons Bryan and her would never work.

Her head she could convince, but her heart?

Another problem altogether.

Chapter Nine

"I can't believe how much she's learned in a few weeks." Jade ran her hand over Teeny's back. Perfect Puppy wasn't as full tonight. Only four other dogs were there. Daylight stretched longer each day, but when she walked in with Bryan an hour ago, the weather had an ominous feel. She glanced up at him. "She actually ignored the treat until you commanded her to take it."

"I didn't think it was possible." Bryan grinned, cell phone in hand. "Let's get a picture for Lucy."

Jade moved next to him and peeked around his shoulder to see the screen. He smelled fantastic, as usual. Masculine. Her mental admonitions to think of him as a friend, one who was moving soon, kept growing weaker.

Last Sunday afternoon he'd taken her to Evergreen Park and taught her how to read a map of the area. She now understood longitude and latitude and could identify major landmarks on the map. They had not entered the woods. He'd kept it businesslike, but she still found herself holding her breath as he traced a pencil over the various areas on the map.

Joining him here with Teeny felt more and more domestic, like it was *their* dog they were training. The worst part? She liked the feeling of being one half of a couple, being able to rely on someone else for a change. Oh, why was she letting herself indulge in these fantasies? No good would come of them.

"Right there." She tapped his arm. "Look at Teeny's face."

Teeny stared up at them, her mouth open and eyes wide. Bryan snapped the picture. "She'll love this one." He quickly texted the photo along with Teeny's progress to Lucy. Then he steered Jade toward the door. "Fill me in on what's happening with the store."

Good. A safe topic.

"Saturday is the grand opening. I can't wait." They made their way to Bryan's truck with Teeny trotting between them. "I'm putting the final touches on the displays tomorrow. By the way, your sister is a genius. Moira's jewelry is sure to be a hit."

"Don't tell Libby. It will go straight to her head."

"Oh, and I've been practicing using the compass when I walk to the park every morning."

"Good. Remember the quadrants and how to determine north. Maybe this Sunday we could try hiking a short ways into the forest."

"Maybe." She climbed into the truck while Bryan settled Teeny into the backseat. When she noticed the sky, she leaned forward for a better look. "What is going on with those clouds? They look angry."

"Oh, don't worry about them." He shut his door and fired the engine. "Just a spring storm. If it gets bad, the sirens will go off."

"Sirens?" She licked her lips as imaginary sirens screeched in her brain.

"They usually go off for a tornado."

"A tornado!" Clutching her seat belt, she tried not to

imagine being alone in the apartment with a twister raging through. Hadn't Bryan mentioned one leveling half the town a few years ago?

Bryan steered the truck to the road. "Relax. This is just a lightning storm. Go to the basement if you're worried. It's the safest place."

Visions of a tree toppling onto her roof made her air supply close in. She yanked at her shirt collar. The dark clouds seemed to roll faster and faster toward them, like dust kicking up from a hundred wild horses.

She wanted to shake Bryan's shoulder and point at the menacing weather, but he was babbling on in that calm voice of his. "Lightning is actually good. It breaks up the nitrogen, which allows oxygen to bond with the nitrogen and form nitrates. They shower the ground below. Good fertilizer. Of course, not everyone believes lightning makes the grass greener…"

"Bryan, I don't have a basement!" The words pelted through the small space.

He stopped talking and turned to her with a stunned expression. "Haven't you ever been in a storm?"

"Yes, of course I have, but not…" She crushed the fabric of the seat belt and averted her eyes. How could she explain? *Not all alone.* Storms in Las Vegas happened, yes, and they could be terrible. But she hadn't experienced one in the country without Mimi in the room next to her.

It had been too long since she'd done any of the steps on her own. Getting over her fear had dropped on her list of importance. After all, Libby didn't like hiking in the woods, and she managed to go about her days just fine. However, Libby probably had no problem driving through all those trees to get out of town, and Jade still hadn't made a solo trip to Kalamazoo. The thought of getting lost or her car breaking down kept her trapped in Lake Endwell.

Online shopping would get old after a while. She'd been relying on Bryan's sturdy presence too much. It was one thing to be near a few trees in a park with him by her side. Another thing entirely to be all alone. Jade pressed her fingertips to her temples and rubbed in a circular motion.

Fat raindrops splattered against the windshield, and Bryan flicked on the wipers, but within seconds, rain pummeled the truck.

How was she going to make it through the night? Whimpering under the covers, most likely. A huge old tree with gnarled branches stood to the left of her store. What if lightning struck it and it fell on the roof? What if it crashed its way inside her bedroom? Reaching for her...

Her heartbeat sped, and her breathing grew choppy.

Lord, I haven't been praying like I should, and I haven't been trying to get over my phobia, but please hear me. Please give me peace.

Bryan set his hand on her shoulder. "You look upset. How about I take you to my place for a while? Sam and I have a basement if the storm gets bad. In the meantime, we can watch a movie."

The instant the words were out of his mouth, Jade let go of her seat belt and heaved a sigh. "Thank you. That would be great."

He patted her arm before returning his hand to the steering wheel. A rock in the middle of a hurricane. Could she protect her heart when she was already way too reliant on him? She doubted it. And for a split second, she wasn't sure why she should.

Why not fall hard for Bryan Sheffield?

Because he's not going to be around. He's never get-

ting married, and even if he changed his mind, you're afraid of your shadow.

The warm, honey-sweet feeling vanished.

That did it. Starting tomorrow, she'd try the next step to overcome her fear. Rainstorms, tornadoes and, eventually, snow would come, and she wouldn't always be able to rely on Bryan. He would be in Canada. If he didn't get the job? He'd grow tired of holding her hand whenever she was afraid.

And she was definitely afraid.

Moving here felt right, but it was all going a little too well. If she didn't stay on guard, she'd be unprepared for when the bad times came. They always came when she least expected them.

Lifting her chin a notch, she took a deep breath. Reminded herself why she moved here.

Open the T-shirt shop.

Overcome her fears.

Find the path God had planned for her.

"Are you comfortable?" Bryan glanced at Jade on the opposite end of the couch. Teeny had sprawled out between them. The dog's hind legs rested on Bryan's thighs while her huge, furry head lay on Jade's lap.

"Yes, very." Jade mindlessly caressed Teeny's ears.

He was spending way too much time with Jade.

What was he supposed to do, though? Drop her off at her apartment with a "You'll be fine," knowing there wasn't a basement for her to find safety? He wasn't in the habit of kicking kittens, and he certainly wasn't going to leave her there, not after he'd witnessed firsthand how devastating a tornado could be. No, he'd done the right thing bringing her back to his place. He'd have to ignore the feelings she kicked up.

But how?

Maybe if he thought about Blue Mountain. Exploring new trails. Ice fishing, cross-country skiing. Salmon and eagles. All things he anticipated.

"She makes a good lap warmer." Jade's white shirt was being covered in dog hair with every stroke of her hand. Teeny licked her chops two times and let out a long, satisfied sigh.

"A heavy one, that's for sure." He swatted her tail out of his way.

"I can't believe you've never watched *Pride and Prejudice*. Keira Knightley is amazing in this version, but I have to admit, I like the BBC miniseries with Colin Firth better. He's the perfect Mr. Darcy…"

Bryan had no idea what Jade was talking about, but he nodded and prepared himself for two hours of sheer boredom. Period movies gave him the creeps. He hadn't watched one in…he scratched his chin…ever. That couldn't be right. He'd watched *Gladiator*. Did that count?

"…and the sets! You're going to love his big rambling house…"

The FBI warning froze on the screen for too long. Several flashes of lightning lit up the front window, and thunder rumbled now and then. Jade didn't seem to notice. Good. Witnessing her fear, like he had in the woods and today in his truck, jumbled up his insides. If boring movies with stiff dialogue made her forget, he'd suffer through it.

"It's starting," she said. "Are you sure you don't mind watching this? We can find something more exciting if you want. I feel bad coming here…"

"This bride movie is fine." He adjusted his legs to get comfortable, but the dumb dog pinned him down.

"Not bride. Pride." She rolled her eyes, shaking her

head. "I wasn't sure if you could get this one streamed. I'm surprised it showed up."

"Yeah, yeah. Let's get it going." A twinge of guilt hit him at how terse he sounded.

"You just wait, Sheffield." Challenge twinkled in her eyes. "You're going to love this."

"Sure. What guy doesn't love olden-day movies where you need a translator to understand what they're saying?"

"Is that what you're worried about?" she teased. "I'll translate it for you. Don't worry."

The movie started playing, and Bryan almost groaned at the opening. "Piano music. Birds. A girl reading. You're right. This is amazing."

Jade drew her lips together and threw a pillow at him. "It gets better."

Bryan grinned. "Oh, yeah. Look, she's walking through a bunch of laundry on the line. Gripping. Way better than an action movie."

"It *is* way better. Wait and see. You'll be crying before the end."

"I'm crying now." He nodded at the television. "Why are they all wearing nightgowns?"

Jade exhaled loudly. And for an extended period. "They aren't nightgowns. That's what people of their station wore back then."

"What did that lady just say?"

"She asked her husband if he knew the house had been let. Like rented or leased."

"I know what *let* means."

"Well, stop talking and you'll be able to follow along."

He almost asked about the bonnets, but he caught sight of Jade's eager face and thought better of it. "I didn't understand anything those three girls said."

Jade graced him with a sweet smile. "Then turn up the volume."

He poked fun as the scenes progressed, but he kept an eye on the weather, too. Surprisingly, he didn't mind the movie, but he wouldn't admit that to Jade. "Um, is this Darcy guy walking through the meadow in a bathrobe?"

Jade had been quiet for several minutes. She lifted a finger, not taking her eyes off the screen. "Shh!"

He grinned, taking the opportunity to study her. She was so utterly into the movie. Her little frown as that Darcy guy made a speech. Her hands clasping over her heart as the girl—Elizabeth? Lizzie? he couldn't remember— kissed his fist. The smallest "Oh" Jade uttered as the movie faded out.

The "Oh" did something to him. Something he didn't like. He dug his fingernails into his thigh.

Jade turned to him with big, expectant eyes, and asked, "Well, wasn't it wonderful?"

"Yes. Wonderful. That's the exact word I would use to describe it."

"They're perfect for each other. Mr. Darcy was lovely."

"Lovely?" Bryan snorted. "Every guy wants to be described as lovely. He barely spoke, and he looked down on her."

"Only at first. And he had reason."

"Yeah. He was a snob."

"You're missing the point. Elizabeth *thinks* he's a snob, but he's really not."

"Well, he'd better be prepared to deal with her family. At least Elizabeth was more levelheaded than the rest of them. The mom was a nightmare."

Jade opened her mouth but shut it, then her face positively lit up. "Either way, they're perfect for each other."

"Yep." He had to get out of the rays beaming from her

face. They were drawing him closer, making him think things, like maybe Mr. Darcy was a big fool and shouldn't have come out to the meadow at the end. He'd get married. Then he'd enter their house a year later and realize the entire place had been packed up. Elizabeth would descend the staircase, a cold look in her eyes.

She'd say something like, "You don't know, do you? You have no clue I'm leaving you."

Just like Abby had done. And Bryan had stood there, the blood in his veins turning to slush.

"Aren't you going to say anything?" Abby had brushed past him. Her with her long brown hair and high-heeled boots. She'd picked up her purse and a suitcase in the foyer. "Of course not. You don't even know Carl came back for me."

Bryan's legs froze, and he'd been unable to piece it together, to untangle his tongue. But then things made sense, the whispers all week in the shop at work, the way none of the technicians would look him in the eye.

"When?" The only word he could form. His life disintegrating before his eyes.

"A week ago." She hoisted the purse onto her shoulder.

"I see."

"Do you?" She let out a fake laugh. "In case you don't, I'll spell it out. I'm done sitting around while you and your buddies watch ball games Friday nights. Go ahead and fish every Saturday morning with your brother. Sell your cars in this rinky-dink town. Just do it without me. I'm moving with Carl."

Her words had spun around him, made him dizzy. He hadn't realized—hadn't added up—that his life was so repulsive to her.

"Why him?"

Her cheeks reddened. "I tried to make this marriage

work. I honestly don't know if you hear a word I say. I'm the only one making an effort at this relationship. I used to think you were uncomplicated, but you're boring, lame."

And he'd spent too many months wondering, if he'd been more complicated would she have stayed?

Teeny yawned and leaped off the couch. Bryan rose, too. "Well, the storm let up. I'll take you home."

"Okay." Her beams of happiness dimmed.

Couldn't be helped. Darcy had it wrong. The man didn't know how much he could lose. Bryan did. And he wasn't losing again.

Jade hopped off her stool at the Daily Donut the next morning. Last night had hammered home the fact she needed to get used to being in the woods on her own. No more depending on Bryan.

"Marie's making honey crullers tomorrow." Art winked, resulting in more creases on an already weathered face. "I'll make sure she saves one for you."

"Mmm, sounds delicious. You might have to save me two." Jade lifted her to-go cup in salute and headed to the door. The sidewalks were still wet from last night's storm. She got into her car parked out front. No reflecting under the gazebo at City Park this morning. The exposure therapy steps she'd handwritten were tucked into her jeans. A reference to the Psalm she'd found last night was scrawled there, too. *When I'm afraid, I put my trust in the Lord.*

Within five minutes, she pulled into Evergreen Park and marched straight to the entrance of the blue path. She sat on the bench in front of the blue spruce where Bryan had taken her the first weekend she arrived in town. Unfolding the paper, she smoothed it out and scanned it.

"Practice relaxation techniques before entering the woods. Right."

Jade scrolled through her phone until she found the directions for two techniques.

First things first. Divine power was available. All she had to do was ask.

Heavenly Father, I need Your help. I'm tired of this fear affecting my life. Please take it from me. Give me strength. And peace.

Not wasting a second, she read through the sequence called Calming Breath. She took a long, slow inhalation through her nose, filling her lungs as step one directed. *Done.* Next she was supposed to hold her breath and count to three. She exhaled slowly while relaxing the muscles in her face, shoulders, neck and stomach.

Jade repeated the process. Her face and neck muscles relaxed easily, but she wasn't sure how to untighten her stomach or shoulders. Why didn't the steps say how?

After trying the sequence five times, her stomach uncoiled. Maybe she could try to walk a little ways in the forest now. She clicked on her phone's voice recorder and took a few tentative steps toward the path.

"I did the calming breath technique, and I'm moving into the forest. I'll try to go six or seven feet." With each step, her calmness dissolved and her muscles tensed. "I'm going to stop a minute and do the breaths again until my stomach stops clenching. At least I'm not gasping."

She paused to inhale, counted to three and relaxed. Birds called to one another as they flew above, and Jade tipped her head back to watch them. A bright red cardinal landed eye-level on a branch ahead. It looked around and flew off.

"I just saw the most stunning bird, a cardinal. Beautiful. Striking crimson with a pointed tuft for a crown.

This park is full of birds singing today. I'm about six feet into the path, and I'm not as scared as usual. I'm going to try to stand here a minute." Jade snapped off the recorder and set the alarm on her watch for one minute. She hadn't moved, but the trees crowded her. Sizzling sensations tickled her throat, and she dared not shut her eyes, certain the trees would envelop her.

God, this isn't working!

She inhaled, but it was shaky. Counted to three. And willed her vision to clear. A tree stood to her left. White bark, little black flecks in it.

It was the same type as Bryan had showed her the day they met. A white birch. She was sure of it. Or wait, hadn't he said something about another tree with white bark?

The leaves. Birch trees had small oval leaves.

Without thinking, she marched off the path through a clump of weeds to touch the bark. Smooth. Peeling. She tore a bit off and smelled.

Slightly minty. This was a birch.

Beep. Beep. Beep. Beep.

"I did it!" She pumped her fist in the air. She'd stood in the woods for a full minute without passing out, hyperventilating or curling into the fetal position.

Maybe she had a chance at beating this thing.

Lord, thank You! Thank You for this success!

Her finger flicked through her contact list until she came to Bryan's number. She almost called him, but the way he'd practically shoved her out of his house last night stopped her.

She wasn't mad about it. He'd been honest with her. Moving to Canada. No dating. No marriage.

She hoped he wasn't aware of her escalating feelings.

If he was, he was being mature, putting the brakes on whatever was happening between them.

Tapping her phone against her chin, she hurried out of the woods to the parking lot. She'd keep this victory to herself. Saturday was the grand opening of her store. She might not have a future with Bryan, but she would do whatever it took to have a future in Lake Endwell.

Chapter Ten

"I need this sweatshirt and this Lake Endwell bag with the swirly words, and, oh, did you see these adorable slacks?"

Behind the counter, Jade straightened promotional fliers and eavesdropped on Sally, Libby and Libby's sister, Claire. Shine Gifts had officially opened at ten this morning, and a steady stream of locals had been in and out all day.

"Yoga pants, Aunt Sally." Libby perused a circular rack of tees in various colors. "No one has called them slacks since before I was born."

"Well, excuse me, Miss Thing." Sally shot a look of long suffering at Libby and continued working her way through the store. "Jade, I notice you have plain shirts here. Do you have designs I can choose from?"

"Of course!" Jade rounded the counter and led Sally to the sitting area where she kept a custom binder of her designs for customers to peruse. Two gray upholstered chairs and a round coffee table were positioned on a fluffy dark purple rug. "Here are some I already made, but if you don't see anything you like, describe what you're looking for and I'll do my best to create it.

We should plan a time to discuss a new logo for Uncle Joe's Restaurant."

"New merchandise for the restaurant? It's about time," Claire said. Her shoulder-length waves were dark brown, but she shared Libby's cornflower-blue eyes. "Jade, would you be able to make a design with penguins? We're opening a new exhibit at the zoo, and I absolutely love the little guys."

"Penguins are cute." Jade selected a different binder and handed it to Claire. "Look through these pictures to see if any work."

The bell above the door clanged and a trio of women entered. Two looked to be in their late fifties while the third was elderly.

"It's so bright in here." The stylish one with khaki capris, a coral blouse and matching lipstick headed straight to the jewelry display. "I hardly recognize it. Remember when this was Barry's vacuum cleaner shop?"

A tall, solid woman with eagle eyes and a short flint-colored comb-and-go hairstyle scanned the place. "Barry was cheap. Awful avocado indoor-outdoor carpeting. Reminded me of vomit. It was dark because he only had a bare bulb hanging from the ceiling."

Jade approached the ladies. "Welcome to Shine Gifts. I'm Jade Emerson. May I help you?"

The older one with papery cheeks smiled. "It's lovely. Just lovely, dear."

"Do you carry onesies?" Eagle Eyes lifted one eyebrow. Everything about her was no-nonsense, including her brisk tone.

"Um…" *Onesies. Onesies.*

"The baby T-shirts with snaps at the bottom."

"Oh, right." Jade laughed, waving. She didn't currently carry baby clothes, but if the woman wanted onesies, she would give her onesies. "I don't have any in stock, but I can order them. What exactly are you looking for?"

Eagle Eyes regarded her a moment. The silence grew charged with tension. Jade held her breath, unsure why. The lady made a sucking sound with her teeth. "Camouflage. My son's a hunter, and my grandson will be, too. I want a saying on it. Something manly. Maybe a reference to the boy's grandpa."

Jade exhaled and pasted on her brightest smile. "Come with me. I have some ideas."

The woman didn't move. "Well, can you do it or not?"

Jade pulled herself up to her full five feet. For some reason, winning this woman over seemed important. "Of course I can."

She nodded. "Okay, then."

"I didn't catch your name." Jade led her to the counter.

"I didn't throw it out."

"I'm sure you don't throw anything out unless absolutely necessary."

"What's that supposed to mean?" Her cheeks flushed.

Jade and her big mouth. She hadn't meant it as an insult. "You strike me as the type of woman who is a good manager and not likely to waste anything."

She harrumphed. "Fay Worthington."

Jade ducked behind the counter for her sketchbook, then extended her hand. "Nice to meet you, Mrs. Worthington. Now, tell me, how old is this child?"

"Call me Fay. And he's not born yet. Due in October."

"How exciting! Your first grandbaby?"

Fay's expression softened as her chin lifted. "Yes. And it's about time. Why the young people are waiting until they're in their thirties to have children makes no sense. I had four strapping boys by the time I turned twenty-eight. Didn't hear me complaining."

"No, ma'am," Jade murmured. Part of her wanted to pipe up and mention how hard it was to find a husband, let alone start a family. And what about the couples who tried and tried, yet struggled to conceive? Having babies these days was hard. Jade shook the thoughts away. "So you're looking for newborn clothes."

Fay nodded. A flash of uncertainty crossed her face. A teeny bit of sympathy washed over Jade. Maybe Fay was nervous about becoming a grandmother.

"Well, it's wonderful you're taking such an interest in this baby."

Fay set her purse on the counter. "I've already told my son not to expect me to drop everything to babysit all the time. And when the boy gets older, they'd better make him mind. I don't want him toddling off the dock while I'm fishing. If they don't teach him to respect the water, I will."

"I don't have much experience with babies myself." Jade tapped her chin. "But I loved spending time with my grandma, and I always listened to her advice. She was the wisest person I knew."

Fay nodded. "Not all grandmothers sit around baking, you know."

"That's for sure. You'll have fun with your grandson. I'm sure you'll have him fishing off the dock with you in no time." Jade grinned. "It's my understanding these little tykes grow out of everything at the snap of a finger. You might want to consider a few different designs in various sizes. That way the baby will have something to grow into."

"I thought that, too."

Jade sketched out three quick drawings all geared toward hunting and fishing, then jotted down clever sayings to print on them. Thankfully, she'd had to come up with quippy sayings on a daily basis in her previous advertising positions. She was practically a pro at it.

Fay pointed at things she liked, made a few suggestions and ordered four baby sweatshirts and sweatpants with matching onesies in assorted sizes. All camouflage, of course. The stylish friend bought two necklaces and a shirt. As the trio left, they chatted about the store and how they would be back.

Libby and Claire hustled to the counter. Both wore matching wide-eyed expressions.

"How did you do that?" Libby jerked her thumb backward at the door.

"Do what?" Jade closed her sketchbook and stuck it on a shelf below the counter.

"Tame Fay Worthington," Claire said. "She's one of the toughest women I know. Honest and hardworking, but I've never known her to buy two of anything, let alone four."

Jade chuckled. "She impressed me. I respect women who say what's on their minds."

"Well, you just did yourself a big favor." Sally plopped three shirts and a tote bag on the counter. "Fay might be a tough cookie, but she'll spread the word about this place. You wait."

"Really?" Jade lifted the first shirt off Sally's pile and began folding it. "I hope you're right."

"Yes, and she's the head of the women's auxiliary at her church. They'll stop in."

Church ladies. The thought gave Jade an idea. "Would you say there's a need for Christian merchandise in Lake Endwell?"

"Oh!" Libby jumped, clapping her hands. "That's brilliant! Of course you're right, Jade. Christian gifts. Here. Absolutely!"

Sally's grape-cluster-shaped earrings swayed as she nodded. "Why hasn't anyone thought of that? This is a church-centered community. Christian gifts would be a big hit."

Jade studied the room. "I could fit a small supply of books in the corner."

"Oh, and pictures, things for the home," Libby said.

"I don't have a ton of space." Jade tried to mentally fit more products along the wall.

"You can always find more space." Claire perused the store. "Shine Gifts. The name says it all. Your light is shining."

Jade now understood how the Grinch felt when his heart grew three sizes. Supportive friends, a successful store opening—what more could she ask for? "Thank you. I appreciate all the ways you've made me feel at home here."

"Aw, honey, we're thrilled to have you."

"Yeah, Jade," Libby said. "And don't forget, tonight we're taking you out to celebrate at Uncle Joe's."

"Dinner is on the house." Sally nodded.

"I can't wait." Jade pulled out a paper bag with the Shine Gifts logo. "Thank you."

She almost asked if Bryan would be there. She had so much to tell him but had refrained from texting or calling him. If not tonight, she'd see him tomorrow for their weekly outdoor session. Maybe this time she would be able to hike a ways in the woods, show him she was getting better.

Better?

She frowned. How many times had she tried to be the girl her boyfriends wanted? Until she got over this incessant need to please the people she cared about, she was in no position to have a romantic relationship. Bryan didn't want one, anyhow.

* * *

"Macy!" Bryan opened his arms wide. It had been a few weeks since the entire family got together for dinner at the restaurant. If it wasn't for his six-year-old niece, he wouldn't bother coming anymore. Strange how he could feel lonely surrounded by loved ones. Macy raced into his arms, and he lifted her high in the air. Her dark ringlets bounced over her shoulders.

"Uncle Bryan! When are you coming over for a tea party?" Her cute lower lip stuck out in a pout, and she ran her bitty hands over his cheeks.

"When would you like me to come over?" He settled her on his hip, her face near his.

"Right now!"

He set her back on the hardwood floors of Uncle Joe's Restaurant. "We have to eat now. How about tomorrow?"

Her face fell, then she brightened. "Okay, but don't bring that big dog."

Teeny chewed one of Macy's Barbie dolls last week. The dog was listening to commands and not running off at every squirrel, but Teeny still destroyed a lot of items. Macy's Barbie was just one more casualty in a long line of destruction.

"I bought you a new Ballerina Barbie," he said. "I'll bring it over when we have tea."

She hugged him. "Are you coming to my recital?"

"What kind of question is that? Of course I'm coming to your recital. I've got to brag to everyone sitting around me that my niece is the best dancer up there."

"You're silly." She giggled and took his hand. "Sit by me."

He wasn't turning down that sweet face. He followed her to the long table set for twelve. The restaurant was busy, but then, Saturday nights were usually hectic. Waiters and waitresses in white polo shirts, jeans and aprons tied around their waists bustled about with trays high in the air. A honky-tonk song played over the speakers, and the room smelled of grease from the fryers. Bryan took a seat facing three sets of glass patio doors. The deck was open, but a cool breeze kept all but two couples inside. Beyond the patio, a strip of lawn led to the lake and a long dock.

Claire and Reed chatted with him a minute before moving to the end of the table with Dad. Tommy and Stephanie sat across from Bryan. Macy wiggled around in the chair to his left, and the one on his right was empty.

Tommy had called him a few times to try to talk him out of Blue Mountain Retreat but for the most part was letting him be. Bryan still hadn't said anything to the rest of the family.

"Just waiting on Libby and Jake." Tommy put his arm around Stephanie, whose baby bump kept growing. "Don't tell me this little imp roped you into anything."

"Nah," Bryan said with a grin. "We're planning a tea party. Tomorrow work for you?"

Tommy exchanged a look with Stephanie. They seemed to read each other's thoughts. A pang shot through Bryan's chest. What would it be like to enjoy that kind of connection with a woman? A wife? Forever?

Jade's smiling face came to mind.

"We don't have plans tomorrow. Come over anytime." Stephanie smiled, resting her hand on her belly.

"How are you feeling?" Bryan nodded at her stomach.

"Great! But I'm always hungry. I'm warning you, I'm ordering the grease platter and I'm not sharing."

"You mean the appetizer sampler?"

"One and the same."

Movement behind him made him peer back over his

shoulder. Jade pulled out the chair next to him. He forgot to exhale.

"Hi. I hope it's okay for me to join you. Libby said..."

"We're celebrating Jade's grand opening!" Libby raced around the table to the chair next to Stephanie, across from Jade. Libby gave Stephanie a quick hug and took a seat.

"I've heard about your store," Stephanie said. "I'm Stephanie. Tom's wife. We're glad you joined us."

Tommy stood to lean over, holding his hand out. "Tom Sheffield. Nice to meet you. The rug rat over here is our daughter, Macy."

Jade stretched her neck to smile at Macy. "Hi there."

Macy brightened. "I'm a ballerina."

"You are? I love watching ballet."

"I'm going to be in a recital, and I get to wear a purple tutu."

"Really?"

Macy tugged on Bryan's sleeve and whispered loudly, "You should bring her to my recital."

He patted her hand and decided not to respond before shifting his attention to Jade. Her flushed cheeks, sparkling eyes and straight hair made his stomach feel funny. "How did the grand opening go?"

"Fantastic! I had a ton of customers. I never dreamed it would go this well."

"That's great."

Her shoulders twitched as if she couldn't contain her joy. "What about you? Any new students this morning?"

"Just the usual. Sam, Beth and Shelby." The three had joked, flirted and barely listened to the lesson he'd prepared. He'd grown terse as the session wore on and almost yelled at them all to go home. Frustrating.

"It's for a good cause," Jade whispered, and sipped her ice water.

"Sure. Beth wore flip-flops today. Who wears flip-flops to hike in the woods? I doubt any of them could build a fire even with waterproof matches. I don't know if it's worth the effort."

Jade nudged him. "It's worth it."

Was it? He glanced at Tommy, who laughed at something Stephanie said. Down the line, Reed and Claire sat shoulder to shoulder. Jake had arrived and Libby swatted at his arm and chuckled, shaking her head at whatever he said.

Yes, it would be worth it to move on. To truly move on with his life.

Bryan trailed his finger down the glass of water in front of him.

Was it really worth it?

The question no longer applied to teaching the class. He recognized that. No, it was more. This was about everything.

The moment felt important—vital—and a choice sprang in his heart.

Was he willing to fully commit to life again?

It would be easy to move away, to not have to deal with these messy feelings he had for Jade. She'd told him they were meant to be friends, but he could no longer pretend he didn't long for more.

"What's the plan for tomorrow?" Jade asked. The restaurant grew louder. Bryan had to lean in to hear what she was saying.

He was so close he could smell her perfume. His fingers itched to trail her cheek, to tuck the strands of cinnamon hair behind her ear, and her animation kick-started his pulse. "Making a fire. If you're interested."

"I'm interested." She glowed under the restaurant lights. "I would love to learn how to make a fire, Bryan."

He couldn't help but wonder what it would be like to practice more than starting a fire. What would it be like to let his attraction grow? Date her? Kiss her?

He'd be smart to keep the fire in the pit, or he would get burned.

Jade traced the *F* and the *M* on the tree at City Park the next afternoon as she waited for Bryan. She'd arrived fifteen minutes early to collect her thoughts. The lake appeared almost turquoise in the blinding sun, and she shielded her eyes to watch the boats zooming back and forth in the distance.

Every day she felt a little more at home here. This town was where she belonged.

Last night Bryan's family had made her feel like one of them, and Sally had surprised her with a big sheet cake with creamy frosting and purple lettering that spelled out Congratulations, Jade! Libby had gone onstage, grabbed the microphone and welcomed Jade in front of the packed restaurant. Jade had to hold back tears as everyone clapped.

These people—these Sheffields—were something.

She'd love to be part of a family like theirs.

Mimi had told her many times that someday the right man would recognize her for the jewel she was and snatch her up. Jade suppressed a sigh. If any guy was going to carve her initial in a tree next to his, she wished it would be Bryan. It wasn't that she needed an adolescent show of affection. She just wanted a great story to tell her grandkids.

But it wasn't going to happen.

She was starting to suspect she'd dated the wrong guys

all this time to avoid getting close enough to have a real relationship. Maybe falling for no-dating-or-marriage Bryan was another way for her to avoid intimacy.

Woof, woof!

Teeny galloped toward her. Bryan had to run to keep up with the dog. They stopped, both of them panting, in front of her. Jade scratched behind Teeny's ears. "What happened? I thought she was getting better at not taking off at a sprint."

"She was. But she must have missed you."

"It's only been a few days."

"Two days too long." His gaze enveloped her. The Detroit Tigers tee fit perfectly—not too tight, just form-fitting enough to hint at his firm muscles. A backpack hung over his shoulders.

Was he flirting?

Of course not. She wasn't a mathematician, but she could add. Bryan plus Jade equaled zero. They'd both said it.

"There's a fire pit close to the lake down there." Bryan pointed to a circle of benches near the water. "I'll gather what we need. You can stay here."

Before he could walk away, Jade said, "Wait, in all the excitement of opening the store, I forgot to tell you. I actually stood in the forest for a whole minute on Friday. Sixty full seconds. And I survived!"

His mouth dropped open. "I can't believe it. You did?" She nodded, gasping when he pulled her into his arms and lifted her off her feet. "I'm proud of you. Wow!"

She could feel his heartbeat through her thin shirt. She'd been correct about his muscles—strong against her—and his hug warmed her down to the tips of her toes. He set her back on her feet, but she didn't move away. No, she stared up at him, noting the appreciation in his sky-blue eyes. If she didn't know better, she'd say he wanted to kiss her.

And the way her pulse had taken off, she definitely wanted to kiss him.

Maybe she wasn't trying to avoid intimacy, after all. Or she was reading way more into the situation than she should.

She ducked her head and stepped back. Why was this man so intent on moving to another country? If she told him she was wrong about being just friends, that she'd lied when she'd said dating him never crossed her mind, would he see he had everything right here?

"Why don't I come with you to gather wood?"

"Are you sure? If it's too much, we can…"

She stretched her arm out to silence him. "I can do this, Bryan. I'll probably still be scared, but I want to try."

Bryan assessed her until, finally, he nodded. "If you want, you can hold my hand. That is, if it makes you feel safer."

Her throat tightened. Why did he have to be so thoughtful?

"It would make me feel safer," she said softly. "Thanks."

A grin spread across his face. "Don't forget you have Teeny to protect you, too."

"Teeny? Protecting? Only if I have the clicker and a pocketful of treats."

"I came prepared." Bryan extracted a bag of treats from his pocket. "Are you ready?"

Bryan took her hand in his. As their fingers intertwined, she leaned her head against his arm a moment. "You make me feel safe."

He squeezed her hand. "You make me feel…"

She waited for him to finish, but he didn't. What did

she make him feel? Why didn't he answer? How could he say something like that and not complete the thought?

"Make you feel?" she prodded.

"Important."

The compliment spread through her like fizz. "One of these days, Bryan Sheffield, you're going to realize what an amazing person you are."

"Sure. You'll see the truth at some point."

"I see the truth."

He turned to her and stared as if trying to memorize her face. "You make me want to believe it, Jade."

"Then...believe it." She lifted one shoulder.

He moved forward, still holding her hand. "If I said you were amazing, would you believe it?"

How she wanted to say yes, but she couldn't lie, not about this. "No."

"Exactly. It's not that easy."

"What happened to you?" she asked. "Why don't you see?"

The vein in his forehead bulged. "I don't deserve the label. I made a mess of my marriage and basically checked out for the past five years. Real amazing."

"You think the divorce was your fault, don't you?"

He didn't answer.

"Maybe you needed to lay low to recover. I've read articles about the most stressful events in a person's life, and divorce is right up there with death."

"Yeah, and maybe I didn't want to face my old class-mates who gossiped about it. Best laugh they had in years. The joke was on me, all right."

"I'm sorry, Bryan. It must have been a terrible time for you."

He kicked at a twig. "The worst part was I didn't see

it coming. I had no clue she was cheating on me. I felt duped. Stupid."

"I can imagine. But she was the one who was stupid. She had you and threw your marriage away."

"I don't see Abby having regrets."

Jade frowned. "Do you have regrets?"

"I don't know. I think we all want to avoid pain in our lives." He tipped his head for them to continue. "Come on. We have better things to do." They strolled in silence until they reached the edge of the woods.

"Are you sure you want to go in there?" Bryan asked.

Now that they were up close to the trees, the familiar tics flooded her body. Blurred vision, shallow breaths, clammy palms.

"Let me practice my relaxation techniques for a minute first." She closed her eyes, concentrating on her breathing, but not losing sight of the fact Bryan still held her hand. After completing the sequence, she nodded. "I'm ready."

They moved into the woods slowly. She tightened her grip on Bryan's hand, but they continued forward until he stopped.

"Here," Bryan said. "Can you take Teeny? I'll grab sticks and kindling."

She glanced back, shocked at how far they'd come. Her tongue thickened and mouth dried, but she held her free hand out to take the leash.

Bryan picked up sticks and bark from the ground. Teeny moved next to Jade and stayed close, seeming to sense her fear. As Jade petted Teeny's head, her tension lowered at the softness of plush fur.

Bryan shoved everything in his backpack and tucked a few thicker branches under his arms. "Are you okay?"

She licked her lips. She probably had a permanent stress wrinkle in her forehead. "Yes."

He slung his arm around her shoulders and pressed his lips to the hair above her ear. "I'm proud of you."

Then he took her hand and led her back the way they came.

Jade couldn't erase the feel of his lips on her hair, and she tried to pay attention to Bryan's fire-making tips, but she found herself fascinated by his broad back, sighing at the sight of the concentration etched in his face, and feeling all jittery as he stacked the sticks they collected.

Bryan was something special, all right, and his comment earlier made her begin to understand why he didn't grasp it. His divorce had torn down his self-esteem.

After her third attempt at starting a fire and this time succeeding, she sat on one of the benches. Bryan lowered his body next to hers. Smoke tendrils curled up to the sky, and low flames flickered through the wood.

"It's kind of funny to have a fire during the day." Her palms hovered above the fire pit.

He smiled, watching her. "Yeah. I like a fire anytime, but my favorite is on a crisp fall night. The stars take up the whole sky, and everything is quiet except for the crackle of the wood burning."

"Mmm, I'd like that." She could picture herself sitting next to Bryan on an autumn evening. Leaning back, looking at the stars. Holding his hand. She trusted him. If she told him about Germany, he wouldn't laugh at her or think less of her. At least she hoped not. "Bryan?"

"Hmm?"

"You asked me a while back if something happened to make me scared of the woods."

"You want to talk about it?" He leaned forward, hands clasped.

She nodded. Her mother knew, of course, and her dad and Mimi, but Jade hadn't shared the details with anyone else.

"When I was little, I had this fantasy of living with my parents, especially my mom. Mimi convinced Mom to let me stay a summer with her in Germany. Mom was doing research, and she'd rented a Bavarian cottage on the edge of the Black Forest."

"Wait," Bryan said. "*The* Black Forest? Isn't that a made-up place in the fairy tales?"

"I wish it was pretend, but no, it's very real. Anyway, I was seven and too young to stay home alone, so Mom arranged for a babysitter. The girl quit at the last minute, and Mom had a hard time finding anyone else to stay with me while she worked. A few times I spent the day at the neighbor's house—they were from England, renting the place for the summer—but the two boys who lived there teased me and played mean tricks on me."

"How old were they?"

She thought back. "I'm not sure. Probably ten, twelve. Anyway, I was miserable. Mimi had flown with me to Germany, stayed a few days and returned to Las Vegas. I thought my mom would see what a good girl I was and ask me to come live with her."

"It must have been hard to be separated from your parents at such a young age."

She nodded, watching the flames. "The kids at school had moms and dads. I wanted a normal family, too."

"I get that." Bryan took a long, thick stick and adjusted the wood on the fire. It sizzled and popped. Orange embers flew into the air. "I wanted my mom back after she died. Resented my friends who had mothers to bake cookies and fuss over them. Aunt Sally has been doing both ever since, but she still wasn't Mom."

A pang of sadness for Bryan touched her heart. He'd lost his mom at a young age. At least she still had hers.

"I realized that summer I was never going to have a normal family like my friends. Mom can't help it—her greatest passion in life is to find a cure for cancer. And she and my stepfather, Gerald, are two of the most qualified people to do it."

"But what about you?" he asked quietly. Compassion shone in his eyes.

She shook her head. "I could never compete with curing cancer, and she always told me the pregnancy had been a mistake."

Bryan made a grunting noise. "Those are tough words to hear, Jade."

She lifted her lips in a quick smile. "I'm fine. Really. And I'm getting way off track. Um, let's see. Someone from the research center called Mom with news on the Saturday before I was flying home. I can still see the way Mom's face lit up. She practically jumped up and down with excitement. She kissed me on the forehead, told me to stay in the house and watch TV while she went to the lab. Said she'd be back in an hour."

The memories sprang fresh, as if they'd happened last week, not twenty years ago.

"She was gone more than an hour, wasn't she?" Bryan placed his hand over hers. Jade nodded.

"I got bored, and I was mad. Mad at not being enough for her to stay. Mad at always being second, third or seventeenth on her priority list. And I took my stuffed puppy and marched outside. The boys were throwing a ball around."

Bryan slipped his hand under hers. It reassured her, helped her to continue.

"One of them said, 'Hey, you want to see Grandmother's house from *Little Red Riding Hood*?' and I shook my head, telling them it wasn't real. They called me a baby and other names. Then one said, 'She doesn't think Red Riding Hood is real. She probably thinks the Black Forest is made up, too.' Well, I knew the Black Forest was real, because Mom told me about it."

"You went with them."

Jade nodded. Bryan dropped her hand, slinging his arm around her shoulders.

"They ran ahead, laughing because I couldn't keep up. As we got farther and farther in, I lost sight of them. I can still hear them laughing."

The slight pressure of his hand on her shoulder steadied her enough to continue. "I ran, but the forest was so dense and the paths twisted, branching off. Night came too quickly, and yellow eyes glowed all around me. Something scratched at the bark. I kept hearing rustling noises and seeing shadows. I cried and screamed but no one came. A local found me late the next day. I was hunched over my stuffed puppy about a mile from Mom's cottage."

Bryan gathered her into a hug, holding her tightly. "I can't believe you went through all that and still moved here. No wonder you were terrified."

"Really?" She stared up through moist eyes. "You don't think I'm a neurotic mess?"

"Jade, anyone who was traumatized the way you were would be terrified of the woods. You were a small child. You should never have been left alone to begin with."

His words snapped the string holding her guilt together, and it tumbled out, disappearing. Bryan was right. She'd blamed herself for years. She'd disobeyed her mom and followed the boys even though she knew she shouldn't trust them.

"My niece, Macy, the one you met last night, is six. Would you think less of her if she got lost in the woods for two days?"

"No!" Jade straightened, but Bryan kept his arm around her. She couldn't imagine anyone luring that sweet child out to the woods.

But I was a child, too. Like her. Small, trusting, but disillusioned.

"How did your mother react?" Bryan caressed her upper arm.

"She yelled at me for not listening, shipped me back to the States with Mimi and has treated me like I'm a disappointment ever since."

"Maybe that's her way of dealing with guilt since she dropped the ball at parenting."

She'd never thought of that before. Could Mom feel remorse over that summer? Was that why she constantly tried to make sure Jade had the right kind of job?

"I don't know. I love my mom, but I gave up trying to be the perfect daughter."

"You don't have to be perfect." Bryan held her close. "Thanks for confiding in me. I wish you wouldn't have gone through that. You're brave."

She wanted to tell him she wasn't brave. She was ordinary, average, but maybe she'd been hiding behind those labels, too.

So many things about her life she thought were true had wiggled off the shelf and broken. She didn't have the energy to examine them all and put them back together. Not now, anyway.

She'd relax in Bryan's arms and figure it out later.

Chapter Eleven

"**Y**ou're sure you don't mind doing this?" Bryan ushered Jade into the aisle of the auditorium Saturday night. The air hummed with the excited chatter of parents and grandparents. Thick red curtains hid the stage, but the only thing he could process was Jade's perfume. It did things to him, things he couldn't fight, like making him want to take her in his arms. He located their seats, and they settled in.

"I love dance recitals." Jade opened her program. "I took tap for a few years when I was young. Putting on my sparkly outfit and tap shoes for the recital was big excitement, let me tell you."

A vision of her as a little girl filled Bryan's head, not helping the possessiveness crowding his heart.

"You must be excited." She squeezed his arm. "What day is the interview again?"

"June 2." The director of Blue Mountain Retreat had called Bryan today at four, requesting an interview. Maybe it was nerves, but he hadn't been as excited as he'd thought he would be when they called. He'd almost dialed Jade's number to tell her, but instead, he'd texted her the news. No sense getting in deeper if he'd be leaving soon.

"Two weeks," she said quietly.

Two weeks. Too soon. "I looked through my checklist of skills to teach. I'm behind."

"You'll be great."

Great? The reality of it was setting in. Could he really move away from Lake Endwell? His businesses? Everyone he cared about?

Could he leave Jade? Spending every Wednesday night and Sunday afternoon with her was intense. He was finding it harder and harder to stay enthused about Blue Mountain.

"Hey." Sam shuffled down the row toward them.

Bryan murmured, "We can talk more later."

"I hear your store is the hit of Lake Endwell." Sam grinned, moving past Bryan to sit. More of the family arrived, chitchatting with him and Jade. Bryan peeked at her profile. Smiling and expectant.

"Having fun yet?" Jade tilted her head close to his shoulder. Her megasmile hit him full force. He froze. This beautiful woman was with him.

And they could only be friends.

Libby waved at Bryan and immediately turned her attention to Jade. "I got your message! The books arrived?"

"Yes, and I love them. I ordered women's devotionals and Christian self-help books. You don't think shoppers will be too embarrassed or intimidated to buy them, do you?"

Bryan tapped the program against his leg. Jade and Libby had gotten close. Maybe that was good. Jade didn't have family around, and she fit in with Libby. Abby had made next to no effort with his sisters.

"Oh, no." Libby flourished her wrist. "You can always

put a sign in front of the display saying Makes a Great Gift. That way no one will know if they're buying the book for themselves or someone else."

"Good idea." Jade shifted to face Libby. "And you think the corner near the door is a good spot? I spent all week filling orders and haven't had time to deal with the books yet."

"Do you want me to stop by Monday night? We can put everything out together."

Bryan almost interjected he'd come over and help, too, but the lights dimmed and everyone hushed. Soon, the recital was in full swing, and four numbers later, Macy appeared with a dozen other little girls in purple tutus.

"She's adorable," Jade whispered, touching his arm. "I want to scoop her up and take her home with me. What a cutie!"

Visions of Jade holding hands with Macy, both of them giggling, came to mind. And another image of Jade, this time holding hands with him as he carried a cinnamon-haired toddler on his shoulders, smacked him square in the chest.

He loved being an uncle, but being with Jade made him want a family of his own.

Squirming, he tried to focus on the girls leaping and bending, but Jade's presence next to him kept bringing him back around to children. Ones he'd never thought he would have. Until...

No. How could he think about this now?

If he started wanting children, it wouldn't be long before he considered all that entailed.

Marriage.

More than friendship.

A life here. Not in Blue Mountain.

He cleared his throat. A beautiful woman with shiny

auburn hair and a short-sleeved bright green dress that perfectly matched her eyes sat next to him. She had a good heart, a kind soul. Even if he wanted to take their relationship to the next level, she didn't want it.

Jade's nose was upturned, her attention laser-like on the dancers ahead.

He couldn't consider it.

Her childhood had left her gun-shy. When she'd told him about being lost for two days and about her mother, he'd wanted to announce he would always protect her, that she would never feel like she was second or third again, she'd never be lost and alone and sad. But how could he make that kind of promise?

He couldn't. He was the guy whose wife left him for a man willing to chase her across the country, one who probably enjoyed fine dining and hated sports.

Jade pointed, giggling at one of the girls whose wand had gotten caught in her hair. He chastised himself to pay attention to the recital. This was Macy's big show.

The rest of the program passed, and the curtains finally closed.

"You're coming to Tom and Stephanie's for ice cream, right, Jade?" Libby asked as they made their way up the aisle.

"Oh, I wish I could," Jade said. "But the baby clothes Fay Worthington ordered came in, and I need to set the designs on them. Plus, I'm trying to get the PTA to order school shirts from me. So far the president has refused to even look at a design. I'm making samples to bring her."

"You'll wear her down. See you in church tomorrow, and don't forget, I'm coming over Monday to help."

They joined the throngs of people in the foyer and hugged and congratulated Macy. Slowly the crowd dispersed.

"I'll walk you to your car." Bryan steered her to the doors. The weather was perfect for mid-May. Warm with a gentle breeze. A full moon illuminated the sidewalk. "You're not too busy for our session tomorrow, are you?"

Her heels clicked on the pavement. "Of course not. I'm catching up on everything tonight. In fact, I have a favor to ask." Shy eyes peered from under her curled lashes.

If she asked him to pull a star down from the sky, he'd agree.

"What is it?" he asked huskily.

"Before you take off for your interview, I want to see your granddad's camping spot. I know I've only been in the woods a little while, but I want to try it. Do you think we could hike there tomorrow?"

He'd never taken anyone there before.

He wanted to take her. "Are you up for it? I mean, if you think you can handle it, I'd like to show it to you."

"Bring Teeny." Jade smiled. "I know it sounds stupid, but having her there makes me feel better about the woods."

"It's not stupid. She's turning into a good dog." He said a silent prayer of thanks for Lucy's overseas adventure.

Jade unlocked her car, and Bryan opened the door for her, waiting until she sat behind the wheel before shutting it and rapping his knuckles on the window twice. She lowered her window.

"Thanks for coming tonight." He bent, inches from her face.

"Thanks for making me feel like one of the family." And she drove away, leaving him staring after her.

Family?

He wanted her to have people to rely on when he moved, but the way she said *family* made him wonder.

Maybe dating him was starting to cross her mind. Or was he reading too much into it?

What if she was part of his family?

His body signals—the erratic pulse, up and down stomach and the inability to look away from her burgundy lips—were anything but brotherly.

He blew out a breath.

Clenching his teeth, he marched to his truck. He'd gotten the interview. Who knew how many other candidates there were? If he was hired, he'd have to leave, have to stop thinking about Jade and forever.

Tomorrow. Hiking to Granddad's camping spot. He could keep this insanity under wraps until he knew for sure if he was moving.

But did he even want the job? Or did he want Jade?

Jade tightened the straps on her backpack and checked her outfit one more time. Hiking boots, jeans, a black tee with gold letters spelling Shine Gifts, her hair in a braid and a GPS watch, just in case. Thankfully, the weather kept growing warmer. There was something about the sun kissing her face. Reminded her of home.

"I think we're all set." Bryan and Teeny stood next to her on the side of old Ranger Road. Bryan had parked his truck in the driveway of a field. Little green shoots popped up in rows of black dirt. Apparently, his uncle owned the property, so they were free to hike for miles.

Hiking for miles.

Didn't scare her the way it usually did, but that probably had to do with the big lug of a dog slobbering next to her and the incredible man by her side. Last night at the recital, she'd let herself fantasize about being Bryan's girlfriend. Attending his family's future events with him. So far living in Lake Endwell had been all about going with the flow, laughing with Bryan at dog training, grabbing a bite to eat after.

She was falling in love with him.

Him. Mr. Unavailable. Soon to be relocated.

Pain streaked through her heart. Why did he want to move? She'd be alone again. Maybe not in body, but in spirit, where it hurt the most. He was the best friend she'd ever had.

Well, at least she still had Libby. They texted every day and chatted about the store. They'd even gone shopping one afternoon. The rest of Bryan's family was welcoming and open, too.

"Okay. This way." Bryan pointed to the field. "We'll go along the perimeter. These are soybeans, by the way. Uncle Joe rents his land out to a local farmer. Next year will be corn. There's not a lot of room, so why don't you follow me. I'll take Teeny."

"Sounds good." She fell in behind Bryan and matched his strides. The ground was soft but not wet, and there wasn't a cloud in the bright blue sky. Butterflies chased one another, and little cotton-like fluffs drifted around them. "What are these white puffy things?"

"Poplar seeds. We call them cottonwood trees. They release their seeds with wispy white threads. I'm surprised they're still flying around. Should be about done by now."

"They remind me of snow, not that I've seen much snow in my life."

He looked over his shoulder and grinned. "Expect that to change. You'll see a lot of snow this winter."

She almost blurted out he'd have to teach her how to make a snowman, but then she remembered he might not be there. What was she going to do without him around?

Mom had called before church this morning. Ever

since Jade had opened up to Bryan about being lost in the forest, she kept coming back to his comment about her mother. Before talking to him, Jade had never considered the possibility that Mom felt guilty about her getting lost, but she'd turned it over and over for days. She'd almost said something to her on the phone but chickened out at the last minute. Maybe some things should stay in the past.

Jade *could* add it to her prayer list. Sally had told her about an experiment some of the church women were doing called prayer walks. Jade had made her own little ritual. On weekdays after chatting with Art at the Daily Donut, she'd begun talking to God as she strolled to City Park. Then, when she got to the pavilion, she'd look out on the lake and listen. Just listen.

It made her feel Spirit-filled. She'd been thinking things like *Take a chance* and *Don't be afraid*.

Bryan reached the end of the field near the woods. He waited for her to join him, then smiled.

Jitters raced up and down her torso. How could her best friend be the most handsome guy she'd ever seen? And did he have any idea how much he meant to her?

"Are you ready? If you want to quit at any point, we'll go back, say the word. But we'll be in the forest a long time. There isn't a quick and easy way out."

"I want to do this. I'm ready."

"Do you want to practice your breathing first?" He studied her.

She nodded. As she closed her eyes and steadied her breathing, she prayed. *God, please bless this walk. Help me overcome my fears and enjoy this. I want to appreciate the place Bryan has told me so much about. Let me see the beauty, not the danger.*

When she finished, she opened her eyes. "Do you mind if I hold your hand again?"

Bryan's blue eyes darkened a shade, and he gently closed his fingers around hers.

"There's a dirt path." He pointed to the obvious trail. "We'll be able to walk on it together. I'll help you over the log to cross the stream when we get there." He motioned for Teeny to go ahead. He kept Jade close to him, their hands swinging slightly as they moved forward.

"This forest has a wide variety of trees. That's a walnut, and some of the pines have been here for decades."

Bryan chattered about birds, weeds, sand in the soil, acid levels—something about rocks and grit—but the farther they got into the woods, the more the tension mounted in Jade's veins. Hot flashes warmed her neck. She had to retrain her breathing several times. About twenty minutes after they started, she halted.

"Bryan?"

"What's wrong? Are you okay?" The concern in his eyes assured her. "How can I help?"

"I'm getting claustrophobic."

He nodded, swinging his backpack off. He unzipped it and grabbed a bottle of water. "Have a drink."

Jade obeyed. Teeny strained against the leash, but Bryan said, "Sit, Teeny," and the dog sat. A line of drool escaped her mouth.

"I think she's thirsty, too." Jade gestured to Teeny. "Did you bring a dish we could fill for her?"

"I did." He took out a collapsible bowl and poured water in it. She lapped it up with loud, greedy slurps.

Rays from the sun slanted to the ground as they bypassed the trees, and the bird calls above were sweet, lyrical. She took in the forest. *Beautiful.* Nothing like the one in Germany. Bryan put his backpack on and was petting Teeny's fur.

"I feel better," she said. "I'm not as scared with you and Teeny here."

He straightened. "Maybe part of your fear has to do with being alone all that time."

Immediately, she thought of the day she recorded herself entering the woods near the lake. How alone she felt. "I think you're right. But it's weird because I'm used to being alone."

"Not in the woods, though." Taking her hand, he began walking again. Teeny's tail wagged ahead of them. He opened his mouth to say something and must have thought better.

"What?" She didn't clutch his hand tightly, the way she had on their previous hike. No, she held it like she would a boyfriend's.

Take a chance, Jade.

As if sensing her thoughts, he firmed his grip. "You said some things that made me wonder if you felt abandoned by your mom. And then those kids left you in the woods." He glanced at her. "I don't know. I think maybe you added those events together and came up with a lie. That you blame yourself for not listening to your mom and for going off with the kids. You were too young to be left alone by your mother. Those boys should never have lured you out there."

Jade stopped. He'd just said out loud what she'd never allowed herself to think.

He wrapped Teeny's leash around his wrist and faced Jade. "You were never to blame."

He understood. She didn't even fully understand, but Bryan did. A tear fell on her cheek, then more dripped down, one after the other. She couldn't stop them. She didn't try. Bryan wrapped his arms around her. She cried into his chest as his words kept repeating in her head.

He's right. I'm not to blame. I could have been perfect and it still wouldn't have been enough for Mom to stay home with me. I still would have ended up alone and terrified in the woods for two days.

He stroked her hair. "I'm sorry. I didn't mean to upset you. I shouldn't have said anything."

Jade jerked her face back. She wiped her tears away with her hands. "Don't be sorry. You're right. I've held the blame for a long time. I've never been able to live up to Mom's expectations, and I got so tired of trying, Bryan. So tired."

He held her, murmuring in her hair, and she pressed her cheek against his chest, comforted by his strength, his protection, his tenderness. If only she could stay right here forever.

Teeny let out a woof as Bryan's fingers trailed over her braid. "What can I do?"

She exhaled. "Take me to the clearing. I want to see it. We've come this far."

He studied her a moment, and something in his eyes made her think he wanted to kiss her, but finally, he took her hand in his and urged Teeny forward.

Oddly disappointed, Jade shut off the revelations. She needed to pray before she could wrap her head around what Bryan helped her see. The fact she'd refrained from kissing him was good. Without his friendship, life would be bleak.

An hour later, Bryan took a drink of water as Jade and Teeny rested on the plaid blanket they'd spread over the grass in the middle of the clearing. A hawk soared above them, looking for a field mouse, rabbit or snake to eat.

This was a place of peace, but emotions warred inside. He tried to make sense of them.

He wasn't a psychiatrist. Had no experience with this sort of thing. But Jade never should have had to carry the burden of her mother's negligence and the cruelty of those kids.

She rested on her side, her arm tucked under her head. Her chest rose and fell softly. He guessed she was asleep. Teeny sprawled next to her, as cozy as could be.

Jade said she'd gotten tired of trying to live up to her mom's expectations. That must be one of the reasons she always deflected compliments and acted like she wasn't special.

Massaging the back of his neck, he frowned. He could relate. A few weeks after Abby left, he'd finally dragged himself out of hiding, thrown on a pair of sunglasses and gone to the coffee shop. A group of married women he'd gone to high school with didn't notice him standing there. They laughed and talked about how women loved bad boys. How good-looking Abby's ex was, and how tempting it would be to get back together with someone like that. He'd paid for his coffee and tried to slip out, but one of them spotted him, and the whole group had fallen silent.

For months customers would stop into his dealerships and, not realizing he'd gotten divorced, ask when he was starting a family. The pity in their eyes when he told them he was single had crushed him.

He'd spent more and more time at home. Closed himself off.

Jade had helped him in so many ways. She'd helped him trust again.

He trusted her.

Her eyelids fluttered, and she yawned, slowly sitting up. "I guess I was more tired than I thought."

"You had an eventful day."

Strands of hair escaped her braid, giving her a rumpled air. He didn't know what was prettier—Jade all dressed up or sleepy. Both.

"About earlier," he said. "Are you okay?"

"I'm glad you helped me see the truth, Bryan."

"You helped me, too." He leaned back on his elbows. "After Abby left, it was easier to withdraw from everyone."

"I understand."

Teeny's legs kicked as she slept. Bryan's eyes met Jade's. They smiled.

"Bryan?"

"Yeah?"

"Was Abby different before you got married?"

He raised his eyes to the sky. The easy silence of the clearing mellowed him. "Not really. We were introduced by mutual friends. She flirted, and I liked the attention. She had good points. She got things done, liked to be in charge."

Jade nodded, encouraging him to continue.

"After we were married, I couldn't please her. She thought I was..." He couldn't bring himself to say it. If he admitted it to Jade, she'd have a label for him.

Her attention turned to her hands clasped in her lap. "You don't have to say more. I know this is painful."

All the vulnerability she'd shared with him in the woods flashed through his mind. It hadn't been easy for her, either.

"She thought I was boring. Her parting words."

"Oh, Bryan." Jade rose to a kneeling position. "She was wrong. You could never be boring." She grinned, her face lighting up. "You know so much about nature, and you make it sound fascinating. You're passionate, and you make me want to see Lake Endwell the way you do."

Her words filled in the broken patches of his heart.

"I didn't know Abby. But I know you. You don't waste words the way more social people do, and I like that about you. I've never met anyone who cared enough to help me the way you have—well, besides Mimi, of course."

"You're easy to help," he said quietly. Her words tore down the remaining fences around his heart. He wanted more. Much more than friendship. "I'm glad we came out here today."

"Me, too." She rotated her neck to take in the view. "I get it. I get why your granddad came here. I feel closer to God. Like He's right here blessing us."

The warm breeze soothed him. He felt it, too. "It's funny, but Granddad always said God loves to bless us."

"I think he's right. I've been praying every day. It's helped me calm down when pressure builds. Dealing with this fear has been a lot of pressure." She closed her eyes.

Bryan held back the words he longed to say. This wasn't the time to make declarations, not when she'd dealt with so many emotions already. He'd have to pray about it first, anyhow. He would not repeat the mistakes he made with Abby. Too much was on the line. More than before.

His heart needed forever this time.

Chapter Twelve

Jade hauled the last box from the back room and placed it next to the shelf Bryan assembled at the front of the store after their hike. The sixth yawn of the hour seized her, and she covered her mouth until it went away. Almost five o'clock—closing time.

She'd barely slept last night. Excitement, relief and pain spun around her for hours after Bryan left. She still couldn't believe he'd cut to the heart of what she'd been too blind to see. The guilt she'd carried—that she was responsible for her mom's apathy and getting lost in the woods—was gone. Completely. But she had a feeling it would take a long time before she came to grips with its effect on her worth.

On the way to the park this morning, she prayed, thanking God for helping her hike through the trees, for showing her she wasn't to blame, for sending Bryan to understand her in a way few people had.

Yesterday she'd thought she was falling in love with him, but she was wrong.

She was already in love with him.

She loved him.

Plain and simple.

"I'm here to pick up my grandson's outfits." Fay Worthington swept into the store and strode to the counter. The door closed behind her with a click.

Jade propped a smile on, hoping she didn't appear as tired as she felt. "They're in the back. Let me grab them for you."

She'd installed metal shelving with handmade alphabet cards to make it easy to find finished orders. After selecting Fay's, Jade returned to the counter and carefully unfolded each tiny outfit.

"What do you think?" Jade held up the smallest onesie with Grandpa's Hunting Buddy embroidered in bright orange.

Fay took it from her and scrutinized the stitching. Turning it over, she stretched the material a few times, then unsnapped the bottom. "I hope this will hold up in the wash."

"I researched the highest-quality suppliers I could find. If you have any problems with the material or workmanship, please return it to me, and I will either replace it or refund your money."

Fay nodded and handed it back to her. "I bought a child's fishing rod. I told my son I'm teaching the boy to fish, and do you know what he said?"

"What?" Jade smiled, hoping it was something good.

"He said, 'Ma, I wouldn't let anyone else teach my kids how to fish.'"

"You're going to be a fun grandma, Fay. Your grandson will probably go around bragging to his friends how cool you are."

Color stained Fay's cheeks, and the woman actually smiled. "I never had much of a relationship with my grandmother. She lived a hard life and didn't have time for nonsense."

"Well, I didn't have much of a relationship with my mother. But I sure had a great one with my grandmother. You won't regret making an effort with your grandson."

Fay nodded, waving at the pile. "Well, let's see the rest."

Jade showed her the other clothes, and when Fay approved them, Jade held her finger up. "I have a surprise for you."

"What's this?" Fay drew her eyebrows together.

She held up a baby-blue T-shirt with *I'd Rather Be Fishing with Grandma* in navy letters.

Fay covered her mouth, her eyes shining bright. Then she grew serious. "I didn't order that."

Jade winked. "It's on the house."

Fay shook her head. "You'll go out of business if you give everything away."

"I'm not giving everything away. I want you to have this. I'm excited for you." Jade wrapped everything in tissue paper, sealed it with a gold circle sticker and placed it in a large cream-and-purple-striped bag.

Fay leveled a serious stare at her. "You've got yourself a good man there."

"Pardon me?" Jade stilled.

"Bryan Sheffield. Stan and I always buy our cars from his dealership. Tom's honest, too, but you can ask Bryan about any vehicle on his lot, and he'll know the answer. Even the used cars. He's a hard worker. Knows his stuff."

"Yes, he's…" Jade couldn't continue her thought. Not to Fay at least.

"He's never overcharged us. Always given us a good deal. You'd be smart to snatch him up. It's strange he never remarried. That disgrace of a wife didn't deserve him." Fay tapped her temple with her finger. "Think about it. Don't let that one slip away. Now I've got to get supper on the table."

"Thank you, Fay. I appreciate your business." Jade normally would follow her to the door, but her feet refused to move. Fay's words whirled in her mind. Fay thought she and Bryan were a couple?

They were friends.

Friends who spent a lot of time together.

They'd been sitting together in church every Sunday for weeks. Spending Sunday afternoons in local parks. Wednesday-night dog obedience classes. The occasional pizza out after.

No wonder Fay thought they were a couple.

The door opened again, and Libby breezed in as fresh as the daylilies blooming out front. "Hey, Jade, are you ready to get the books displayed?" She dumped her oversize tan leather purse on the counter, rubbed her hands together and made a beeline to the boxes.

"Libby?" Jade chewed her bottom lip and joined her.

"Hmm?"

"Fay was just in, and she was under the impression Bryan and I are a couple." She let out a nervous laugh.

Libby tossed her blond hair over her shoulder as she poked through the top box. "Well, aren't you?"

"Uh…"

Libby straightened. "What's going on? Don't you find Bryan attractive?"

"He's unbelievably gorgeous, Libby, of course I find him attractive."

"So what gives?" With her index finger, Libby beckoned her and sat in one of the chairs. "I haven't seen Bryan like this. Ever."

"What do you mean?" Jade took the other chair, propping her elbow on its arm and letting her chin drop onto her fist. "He doesn't seem different to me."

Libby chuckled. "You didn't know him before you moved here. He was—well, I don't know how to describe it. It was as if a cloud had permanently covered him. Not that he was ever very social, but he kept to himself."

Jade thought about it. Bryan seemed introverted, so that didn't surprise her.

"Since you came to town, the brother I grew up with is back. Bryan always bought me candy and played board games with me. He protected me more than my other brothers. Didn't say much, but he always seemed to know what was going on. I'll never forget when Mitch Waverly showed up an hour late for a date—I think it was my senior year. Anyhow, Bryan was over, watching television with Dad, and after ten minutes ticked by Bryan waited in the driveway with his arms crossed over his chest like a bodyguard. When Mitch finally showed up, Bryan hauled him out of his car by his shirt and lectured him about the importance of being on time."

Jade's jaw dropped.

"Yes, I know." Libby laughed. "Then Abby left him and the spark in his eyes disappeared. I'm thankful he met you."

"I wouldn't have had the courage to move here if it wasn't for his outdoor survival class. When I saw it offered on Lake Endwell's website, I immediately went ahead with my plan. Called Mrs. Reichert about the building I saw online. Everything fell into place because of Bryan."

"See?" Libby smiled, snapping her fingers. "It was meant to be. Pastor Thomas would tell you God had His hand in it."

God definitely had His hand in it. "I'm happy here.

Love this little store and the town. The lake is so incredibly beautiful. I walk over to City Park every morning before I open shop."

"And Bryan?" Libby asked.

Jade paused. She didn't have the answer. She didn't fully understand the question.

"Bryan is one of my best friends." *My best friend. I couldn't bear to lose him.*

"Just a friend? Nothing more?"

Jade shrugged. She couldn't tell Libby about Bryan's plan to move. Sharing his secret was his responsibility, not hers. "Neither of us is ready for much right now. I'm still finding my way with the business, and he's been honest about not wanting to remarry."

"I don't get it. Why wouldn't he get married again?" Libby crossed one leg over the other. "Anyway, I see how he is with you. Maybe you've changed his mind."

Jade shook her head. She'd donate a kidney to change the topic.

Libby frowned. "I never got the impression he and Abby were soul mates, but I'll be honest, I was kind of self-absorbed when they were together. He looks at you the way Reed looks at Claire and Tommy looks at Stephanie."

"I don't know about that." Jade averted her gaze.

"I do. I think you should go for it. You won't find a better guy than Bryan. Trust me."

Words stuck in Jade's throat. She wanted to tell Libby she was right. Jade would never find a better guy than Bryan. But he was leaving. What good was the perfect man if he was hundreds of miles away and refused to date anyone, including her? "Bryan and I are good friends. I don't want to lose that."

"You wouldn't. He's loyal."

Jade scrambled to counter Libby's line of thinking. "Okay, but what if we dated and realized we weren't right for each other? Breakups are messy. I *would* lose his friendship, and I'd also lose yours. You mean too much to me, Libby."

Libby covered Jade's hand with hers. "No matter what happens, we'll always be friends."

"You can't really promise that."

"I can. Claire taught me not to let circumstances affect friendships. Never let that worry get in the way of what could be."

Jade's throat tightened even more. The hurdles she'd placed on the path to Bryan were being knocked down one by one. But the big one remained: Canada.

If she and Bryan were meant to be together, wouldn't they be together here? Jade belonged in Lake Endwell. She was certain of it.

Did Bryan really want Canada?

Or did he want to be anywhere *but* Lake Endwell?

Jade didn't know. But she wasn't leaving. Not when she finally had the life she always wanted.

Friday night Bryan checked the clouds rolling in rapidly. Everything in his life seemed to be moving too fast. Jade had seemed uncomfortable at Perfect Puppy the other night, and she'd vetoed their usual pizza after. Maybe it was for the best. He needed to concentrate on the upcoming interview. "Looks like a storm is on its way. Let's get a fire started and make a shelter."

"Or let's go back to the house." Sam yanked his thumb back toward the yard. "This is not my idea of fun."

"Come on, man. You gave me your word." Bryan pushed through the brush in the woods behind their bungalow. Last night he'd asked if he could teach Sam a basic survival class. Sam had grudgingly agreed. "Grab as many sticks as you can for kindling. I'll chop a few saplings down to make a lean-to."

"You already know how to do this. I don't know why we're out here."

Bryan let the small hatchet in his hand drop next to his leg. "You're really going to bail on me? I'm asking for two hours."

Sam crossed his arms over his chest. "Why?"

"Why what?"

"Why me? Why now?"

"I told you. I want to be ready for the final class tomorrow."

"Yeah, and Beth and Shelby won't ever be making a fire or a shelter in the woods, so I think you're okay there. What's the real reason you're obsessed with dragging me out here?"

Bryan swung the hatchet against the base of a slender maple without any leaves. "This is a good tree to cut down because it's dying, anyway. It won't compete for sunlight or nutrients with healthy trees if we use it for firewood."

Sam opened his mouth, then closed it. With a grunt, he collected twigs. "You didn't answer my question."

Bryan hacked at the trunk.

Sam moved next to him, crowding him. "Can you just give me a straight answer for once in your life?"

"What are you talking about?" Bryan slowly turned to face Sam.

"You've been giving Jade private lessons for weeks."

"What does Jade have to do with it?" He tightened his hold on the hatchet. "Just gather the wood."

"I know I'm not Tommy, but would it kill you to confide in me?"

Confide in him? Uneasiness trickled down his spine. Had Sam found out about Blue Mountain Retreat? If yes, how? Tommy could have blurted it, but Bryan doubted it. That left Jade. "I don't know what you're talking about."

"You've been dating Jade, yet you don't talk about her at all."

He searched Sam's face and all he saw was hurt. Sam clearly didn't know about the job. Bryan shouldn't have questioned that Jade would say anything. Sam was asking about Bryan's love life—what a joke that term was.

"I'm not dating Jade."

"Sure. You're not dating her." He shook his head, scoffing. "We live together, Bry. When are you going to wake up and realize I'm more than your nuisance of a little brother? I'm tired of being second best to Tommy."

Bryan blinked. "When I say I'm not dating Jade, I'm telling you the truth."

But he wasn't telling Sam the entire truth. He hadn't told him about Ontario.

"For someone not dating, you two have a funny way of showing it. Dog classes, sharing a pew in church, your private lessons—whatever that means. You're dating her. Why won't you admit it? Or is it only me you won't admit it to?"

Bryan chopped the hatchet into the ground and straightened. Didn't Sam know how much he cared? He thought much more of him than as a pesky brother. Yes, they teased each other, but…Bryan had never been good at showing it. Never gotten around to saying it, either.

"Jade and I are friends."

Sam snorted. "Yeah, right."

Bryan cracked his knuckles. It was time to come clean with Sam. About moving. About why. "You're one of the few people I can trust to be honest with me."

"Really?" Sam shifted his weight to his other leg.

He nodded. "I applied for a job in Canada as an outdoor guide. The interview is June 2. I've been teaching the class for experience."

"Canada? You're not serious."

"I am."

"Why?"

Bryan shrugged. "It's too hard. Living here is too hard."

"No idea what you mean." Sam leaned his shoulder against the trunk of an oak.

"I'm never going to have what they have."

"Who?"

"Tommy, Claire, Libby. I tried it once." He wanted to try it again. He wasn't ready, though. Needed time to think about it, to figure it out.

"Yeah, with Abby the Barbarian. What about Jade?"

"What about her?" Bryan picked up the hatchet again and wiped the blades off on the side of his jeans.

"You could have it. With her."

"No." The wind had picked up. Bryan lifted his backpack and hoisted it on his shoulder.

"So let's leave Jade out of the equation for now. You have the dealerships, and you have us. There's no need to move."

Bryan took a step on the path that led back to the yard, but Sam clamped his hand on his arm. "If this is about needing a career change, teach another class here. You're the master of the outdoors. You could win one of those reality survival shows, you're that good."

"You think so?" His chest expanded at his brother's confidence.

"Yeah, I think so. I don't get why you don't see it."

Bryan paused. He'd liked himself until Abby left him. Abby had been wrong about a lot of things. Maybe she'd been wrong about him, too. "I didn't like myself after the divorce. It was humiliating."

Sam frowned but nodded. "I guess I didn't realize. I was away at college at the time."

"I got wrapped up in my own problems. Didn't make an effort with you. You've grown up. You're exactly what Sheffield Auto needs, and I think it's great you opened a new dealership. It took guts to do that."

Sam nodded, his gaze to the ground.

"I'm proud of you, and you *are* one of my best friends. Never doubt that."

"I've always looked up to you, Bry."

Bryan gave him a quick hug, patting his back. "How would you feel about taking over one of my dealerships?"

"No, thanks. My hands are full. And you're not leaving." Sam pointed at him. "You have Jade."

"I don't have Jade, and I am leaving. If they hire me."

"Sure." He flashed a teasing grin. "When's the wedding again?"

"I told you I'm not dating her. She wants to be friends."

"She doesn't act like she put you in the friend zone," Sam said. "Do you know how to read a woman's signals anymore? I'm going to have to teach you everything, aren't I?"

A crack of thunder made them both jump. The dark clouds opened and spilled the rain.

"Let's skip this and grab some hot wings at Uncle Joe's." Bryan grinned.

"Okay," Sam said. "But you're going to have to let me give you pointers on how to read women."

"You're on."

"And don't be surprised when I convince you Lake Endwell is where you belong."

He had a feeling it wouldn't take much for Sam to convince him.

* * *

"Look at that! I didn't know flowers could grow in a lake. Oh, what is the blue bug over there?" Jade faced Bryan in the canoe Sunday afternoon. The sun soared high in the sky, hot and bright, the way she liked it. They couldn't have asked for a better day to paddle on the lake. She'd never been in a boat, much less a canoe. The skimming movement relaxed her.

"It's a dragonfly. They come in different colors. And the flower is a lily pad. They pop up white or lavender. At dawn and dusk, you'll see frogs sitting on the pads. You'll hear them croaking, too."

"Beautiful." She noticed a flat black beetle whose legs skimmed the water like a windshield wiper. "That bug is swimming! Tell me it's not a cockroach."

"It's not a cockroach. It's a water bug." He chuckled, his strong arms rowing side to side. She admired his muscles flexing under the navy blue tee he wore with tan shorts and running shoes. She couldn't see his eyes hidden behind dark sunglasses, but the tiniest sigh of longing escaped her at the way his dark blond hair slightly dipped above his forehead. Hair gel hadn't completely tamed it.

She'd taken extra care with her outfit, selecting cute dark gray shorts that made her legs look longer and a turquoise T-shirt. Her earrings dangled matching turquoise rocks.

"Want to try?" He nodded at the oar attached to the side. "You'd have to face the other way to stay in sync with me."

She grimaced. "I'll tip the boat over if I stand up."

"I've tipped it before. It's part of the experience."

But it would ruin her hair. She'd spent thirty minutes straightening and spraying it. Today she wanted to look her best. If she only had another week until Bryan left for the interview, she would at least leave him with a good impression. Maybe it would change his mind. "I'll row another time."

"Let me know on the way back."

They passed a fishing boat with a man standing, casting a line. "I've never fished before."

"This time of day isn't the best for fishing. Perch, bluegill and trout bite more in the morning or at dusk. We catch a lot of smaller fish off Granddad's dock."

"Do you have to touch anything gross?" She let her fingers trail in the water as Bryan switched sides paddling.

"Night crawlers. They're slimy. And you have to watch the scales when you get the fish off the hook. They can be sharp."

"Um, maybe I'm better off staying ignorant of the process."

He laughed, continuing to row. "I'd bait the hook for you and take the fish off, too. Did it a million times for Libby."

"I knew I liked her for a reason." Jade grinned. "But someone else will have to help me, or have you forgotten you're going to Blue Mountain soon?"

The smile slid off his face. He looked backward over his shoulder and steered the canoe toward shore. They'd glided into a large, private cove. "There's a beach here. Aunt Sally is friends with the owners. They don't mind if we use it."

"Did you know your aunt brought me dinner several times? She'll stop in and say, 'Hon, I saw the light on and figured you were hungry.' She'll chat a minute, hand me a bag full of the most amazing food and leave. Who does that? I love her."

He stared a moment too long. Did she have something

in her teeth? But he cleared his throat and gave the oar two more strong shoves. "Yeah, she's special."

Normally she and Bryan conversed easily, but something was different today. An odd tension crackled between them, and she didn't like it. It made her all fidgety. Pushed her to talk too loud. And Bryan was acting… strange.

"Wait a minute for me to drag the canoe to shore." He took his shoes off, jumped in the shallow water and dragged the canoe onto the sandy beach. "Okay, climb over, and you won't get wet."

He held his hand out. She tentatively stepped over the bench, keeping her balance as the canoe wobbled, and placed her hand in Bryan's. He lifted her out of the canoe and set her on the beach.

The warmth of his body inches away emanated to hers, and he didn't let her go. No, he stared at her with an intensity that only increased the chaos in her mind. Her pulse sprinted as he slowly caressed her bare arms. She should pull away. Or rest her cheek against his chest. Invite him to kiss her?

They both stepped back at the same time. She let out a nervous laugh. Bryan began rubbing the back of his neck, his face burning.

She wasn't the only one affected by the moment.

"It's warm out." She fanned herself. "Mind if I sit on the beach?"

"I'll join you."

They strolled beyond the canoe. Lowering her body to the warm ground, Jade swiped her hand across the sand. "This isn't sand at all!"

He let a scoop of it sift through his fingers. "Shells, rocks, pebbles—there's sand here, too."

She kneeled to peer at the beach. "Oh! These look like tiny snails!"

"Exactly. You'll see a lot of snail shells in the sand here. They like cold water with vegetation."

Swiping a handful, she poked at the assortment of small particles mixed with larger rocks.

"This one is unusual. What do you make of it?" Jade held a flat gray stone between her finger and her thumb. "It looks like a quilt or something."

Bryan leaned in, his breath warm against her cheek. "You found a Petoskey stone. We don't see a lot of those around here. Keep that one. It's the state rock."

She slid it into her pocket. The odd tension between them vanished when Bryan talked about nature facts. She didn't want to explore the emotional side of their relationship, not when time was running out.

"Jade?"

Something in his tone made her think he didn't want to focus on snails or rocks or insects. "Yes?"

His eyes darted side to side, and his fingers tapped against his leg. A sinking sensation slid down her throat. If he was nervous, it meant nature wasn't on his mind, which meant…

Not now. Not here. She needed clarity before he brought up the subject of *them*. What if he gave her some speech about how it had been nice but this was the end of the line?

Or worse.

What if he kissed her?

She'd be lost. She'd kiss him back, put her heart in jeopardy. Put her dreams on the line.

"Oh! What is that?" Scrambling to her feet, she hustled to the edge of the water, where waves gently lapped the shore. A moment later, she sensed Bryan's presence behind her. All she had to do was take the slightest step back, and she'd be in his arms.

His hands closed lightly around her biceps, and he turned her to face him. The intensity from earlier had magnified. His jaw and cheekbones jutted, but not in anger. No, it definitely wasn't anger in his gaze.

He ran the back of his finger down the length of her hair, then lifted his hand to her cheek. His other one crept behind her neck, and he pulled her to him. Lowering his head, he brushed his lips against hers.

Delicious shock rippled through her. He pressed on her lower back, closing any gap between them. And he kissed her. Fully. Completely.

Kissing Bryan was the most natural thing in the world. He felt strong, warm—like the comforter she snuggled into each night, except a million times better. She'd fantasized about being held in his arms, but she'd never imagined them feeling so right.

He backed away from the kiss but kept his arms twined around her waist. She rested her cheek into his chest, not wanting the moment to end.

Standing in his arms was the safe place she'd longed for since losing Mimi.

But it wouldn't last. It couldn't last.

He was set on moving. She was staying here.

She shifted away from him, unsure what to say, what to do. "We can't do this, Bryan."

"Why not?" His low, raspy voice didn't relieve her.

"Your interview is in a week."

The muscle in his cheek flickered as he gazed upward.

"It's important to you." Jade knew this day was coming. She'd known it from the instant he mentioned Canada when she agreed to spend Sundays with him. His kiss sealed the end. The hair on her arms rose. "You'll get the job. And you'll be gone."

"What if I don't go?" His eyes darkened to the shade of a storm.

"Come on, Bryan." She shook her head. "You want it."

"I did." He blew out a breath full of frustration. "I don't know anymore."

"I'm not going to stand in your way. It would be a mistake for you to blow off this opportunity."

"What if I don't get the job?"

Blackness fell over her heart, which was ridiculous due to the perfect summer day. But how was she supposed to take that question? If he didn't get the job, he might be willing to explore a relationship with her?

"You've been clear all along on two things. You're moving, and you aren't dating."

He narrowed his eyes. "And you've been crystal clear that we're just friends."

"What do you want?" Jade shifted her weight to one hip. "You kissed me, knowing full well you plan on moving to Canada. I love Lake Endwell. I'm happy here. If you need to move, I get it, but I don't want to be your backup plan."

"How can you say that?"

"Because it's true."

Hurt flashed in Bryan's eyes, but she couldn't—wouldn't—feel guilty. She twisted, unable to face him a second longer. Her mouth tasted of copper at the thought of being his second choice.

Just once in her life, she wanted to be someone's first choice.

Chapter Thirteen

"I don't know what to do," Bryan said the moment Tommy opened the door.

"Let's go out back." Tommy ushered him down the hallway. "Be quiet, though, Steph is sleeping."

Bryan followed him past the living room where Stephanie curled on the couch with a bright red blanket over her bulging belly, out through the sliding patio door. He hunkered down on one of the cushioned lounge chairs. The late-afternoon sun blazed on the concrete, and Tommy cranked an umbrella to cover them both before sitting on the lounge chair next to him.

"What's going on?" Tommy asked.

Bryan tried to put it in words, but couldn't. After he'd kissed Jade, which had been revealing in a way he hadn't expected, he hadn't been prepared for her reaction. All he wanted to do was stay here, explore whatever was between them, but she'd pushed him away.

When she'd accused him of making her his backup plan, he'd emotionally shut down. They'd canoed back to Granddad's cottage in silence. Sam and his old friend from high school stood on the deck, shouting they were going fishing and for him and Jade to join them. Bryan had waved them off. How could he fish when his life made zero sense? Jade's spine had been rigid and her face pale all the way to her apartment. She'd slammed his truck door shut without a backward glance.

He'd driven straight here.

"How did you do it?" Bryan finally asked. "How did you get the guts to try again with Stephanie?"

A flash of understanding crossed Tommy's face. "Ahh, that's tough. Is this about Jade?"

Bryan nodded.

"I'm not going to lie, Bryan, it was hard at first. I tried to protect myself from falling in love. You of all people know the burn of rejection."

"You can say that again."

Tommy chuckled. "But I'd changed. I'd grown into the man I was supposed to be, and Stephanie had changed, too. We talked with brutal honesty. That kind of honesty freed me."

Bryan thought about his conversations with Jade, how he'd opened up about painful things and she hadn't judged him. She'd also allowed him to speak frankly with her.

"It's funny, but one of those early days when I'd just learned about Macy and had no intention of making a future with Stephanie, Claire said something that stuck with me."

Bryan arched his eyebrows for him to continue.

"She said Aunt Sally told it to her."

"Well," Bryan said. "Are you going to tell me or not?"

"Let me ask you a question first. Do you believe you're divinely guided?"

He thought of all his prayers, of going to church, of his Bible at home. "I guess. Depends on what you mean."

Tommy raked his hand through his hair. "Do you believe life is a bunch of coincidences or not?"

"I've seen too much evidence in my own life that couldn't be described as coincidences."

"That's what I thought, too. And Claire said, 'You'll always take the right turn in the road.'"

Bryan swung his legs over the side of the chair to face Tommy. "Abby was a wrong turn. A dead end."

"I didn't say everything will be perfect. We've got free will, man, and I know I've messed up a lot by ignoring my conscience."

Bryan clenched his jaw. Tommy was right. No one had forced him to marry Abby. He could have worked harder at their marriage. Could have made reservations at those restaurants she liked so much. But he hadn't. "I get what you're saying, and I agree, but what about all the things beyond our control? The bad things like catastrophes and war and sickness?"

"Result of a sinful world. I've been reading the Bible every day for years. God spells it out that we're going to have trouble in this life, but He overcame it for us. He works things out for our good."

"All things? I don't know. It's hard to believe all things can turn out good."

He shook his head. "I didn't say He works things out *to be* good. He works them out *for* our good. Big difference."

Bryan pondered the words. The most painful time in his life was the confusion he felt never being able to please Abby, and when she was unfaithful, confusion became devastation. But he hadn't been walking a close path with God before the divorce. After? Church became more than a habit. It became a necessity.

God *had* used something terrible for Bryan's good. His faith was stronger than it had ever been.

"You and Jade seem to have a lot in common." Tommy leaned back in his chair. "She seems right for you. Don't be afraid to take another chance."

A chance. That's what he thought he was doing when he applied for the job. "The interview is a week away."

Tommy shrugged. "Don't go."

He made it sound easy. "What if I take a chance on Jade and lose?"

"At least you tried. What if you don't tell her how you feel?"

"I move."

"Sounds like losing to me."

Seemed either way he'd lose. Unless… Bryan wouldn't know for sure until he prayed about it.

"Yes, the store is doing well, Mom." Jade wiped her forehead, desperate to end this conversation. All she wanted to do was climb into bed, although it wasn't even dinnertime, and pretend things hadn't changed between her and Bryan. Escape through sleep.

"Have you made any friends?" Her mother sounded concerned.

"Yes, I made friends." She tried to keep exasperation out of her tone but failed. "Libby has been helping me with displays. And the Sheffields have gone out of their way to make me feel at home here."

"Who are the Sheffields?"

Jade never shared much with her mom, and she didn't want to discuss Bryan. This happy time in her life wouldn't continue indefinitely. It had about a week left.

"I took some outdoor classes. Bryan's my instructor. Libby's his sister."

"Oh."

What did that *oh* mean? She hadn't told Mom about the outdoor classes, either. "I never really got over my fear of the woods. When I moved here, I decided to give it another shot."

"And the fear? Is it gone?" She could barely hear her mom's quiet words.

"Yes. I actually hiked with Bryan last week." Jade tightened her hold on the phone. Something inside her urged her to continue, to broach the subject neither talked about. "He helped me see my fear wasn't merely about trees. I think I blamed myself for getting lost in Germany."

Jade waited for Mom's response. And waited.

A muffled sound came through. "I've asked myself so many times what kind of mother leaves a seven-year-old alone in a foreign country. You will never know how terrified I was while you were lost. We had search parties and police. I've never been fit to be a parent, Jade."

Her chest tightened. "It's in the past, Mom."

"I know, but you wouldn't look at me after they found you. You were in the officer's arms, clinging to that dirty stuffed animal. You kept asking for Mimi. I didn't know what to do. I didn't reach out and take you in my arms. The pregnancy was a mistake..."

Adrenaline shot through her veins. "Mom, I'm tired of hearing I was a mistake."

"I never said *you* were a mistake."

"Well, how else am I supposed to take it? You've said it over and over. I get it. You didn't want me."

"It's not that I didn't want you. I didn't want children. Thought you'd interfere with my research."

"Yes, nothing must interfere with your research." Jade barked out a hollow laugh. "It's fine. You got to research, and I got a grandmother who loved me. Mimi took good care of me. I loved her very much." Jade swallowed the thickness in her throat. Her childhood had been happy with Mimi. Not perfect, but it wouldn't have been perfect being raised by her parents, either.

Silence stretched.

"Mom, I wanted *you*. Not Mimi. You. But you refused. I've always wanted more from you than you've been willing to give."

"I know." Her mother sighed. "I…I do love you, Jade."

She'd never heard those words from her mother. They would have meant more twenty years ago. She and Mom had been tiptoeing around the truth for a long time, and now that they'd addressed it, bitterness crept into her heart. She'd never allowed herself to be angry about her mom, just made excuses for her, told herself she wasn't good enough, couldn't live up to Mom's expectations.

She'd always been good enough. And she didn't want to close this cracked open door with her mother, but she wasn't going to pretend everything was fine when it wasn't, either.

"Mom, I'm hurt it's taken twenty years for you to say those words, but I want you to know I love you, too."

"I understand."

"I want something real with you, but only if you can accept me for who I am, not who you want me to be."

Her mother took a sharp breath. "You've accepted me, warts and all. I will try harder."

"Thanks."

They hung up, and Jade sank into her couch, clutching a furry throw pillow to her chest. What had just happened? Mom? Admitting responsibility for her disappearance? Telling her she loved her?

Why didn't it matter as much as Jade had hoped it would?

Maybe because she had something bigger, something more than any person could give her. She had a Father she could confide in anytime, night or day. One who loved her. One who laid His life down for her.

She curled onto the couch, her mind swimming with the complications of the day. Mom.

Bryan. That kiss.

Her breathing came in quick gasps. Her hands felt clammy.

What on earth?

She wasn't anywhere near the woods, so why was her body reacting this way?

God, I'm confused. I don't know what to do. I want Bryan as more than a friend or boyfriend. I want forever.

Jade put her fingers to her lips. She didn't know if she was a candidate for that kind of commitment. And she might not have the courage to find out.

Bryan whittled a stick in his backyard. Teeny lounged on the grass near his feet. As soon as he'd left Tommy's, he'd gone out back and secured the dog to a long leash tied around a strong oak tree.

Jade's words kept hitting Bryan in the gut. Why would she think she was his backup plan?

Because she kind of is.

He scraped his knife along the stick. Wood shavings piled on the ground.

Maybe he needed to analyze his options. On the one hand, Blue Mountain offered a change he thought he wanted. A new job doing something he liked, a fresh start in a breathtaking area of the world and a way out of the desperation he'd sunk into. Whenever he thought of the Canadian village, he wanted to explore the area, do something new. Blue Mountain would be filled with adventures, an outdoor life he would enjoy.

But on the other hand, Lake Endwell was home. He thrived on running his dealerships and the challenges they presented. He spent a lot of time with his family. Adored his niece. Even liked Teeny.

None of the above mattered all that much, though.

The real reason his stomach was churning and the stick was being whittled to a toothpick lived in a small apartment over the old record store.

He wanted Jade.

And he'd continuously put off the one thing necessary to move forward.

Prayer.

He wasn't sure he was ready for God's answer on this. What if God said no? But what if He gave him the go-ahead?

Both made his palms sweat. Risky.

Tommy was right about trying. It was better to try and fail than to not try at all.

He stabbed the stick into the ground and brought his hands together.

Lord, I humbly come before You today with a request. Make it clear to me what I should do. Do I tell her how I feel? Or follow through with my plans? Lead me to do Your will.

A trio of images rolled through his mind. Libby and Jake holding hands at the front of the church. Claire and Reed walking up the aisle. Tommy and Stephanie dancing with Macy at their reception.

Three weddings. Happy weddings.

He frowned. He'd been married, too. Didn't mean the story ended in happiness.

Another picture flashed. Jade laughing in delight as she pointed at the dragonfly this afternoon.

Are You saying I can be happy, too?

Woof. Teeny wagged her tail. Looked like she was smiling.

Didn't get clearer than that.

Jade was it. She was right for him. She was *his* definition of happiness.

Bryan jumped to his feet and began to pace.

How was he going to tell her? He needed to do it right. He'd messed up earlier with the kiss. This time he was planning his move. Writing down everything he needed to say.

He had to make her understand she was his first choice, that she was nobody's backup plan.

His cell phone rang. "Hello?"

Dad barked, "It's Sam. He's been in an accident. Meet us at the hospital. They had to Life Flight him."

Chapter Fourteen

Bryan clutched a foam cup of coffee and willed his eyes to stay open. Libby and Tommy slumped in chairs around the table in the hospital cafeteria. All three of their cell phones were laid out in front of them, ready to grab the minute Dad texted or called. The cafeteria was quiet. The abundance of potted trees reassured Bryan for some reason.

They'd paced the waiting room carpet all night with the rest of the family. Claire, Reed and Jake were waiting upstairs with Dad. Stephanie stayed home with Macy, but she texted Tommy every ten minutes. The stale air and hushed conversations upstairs had driven Bryan crazy, so he came down here. Apparently, Libby and Tommy felt the same since they joined him.

What if Sam didn't make it? Bryan's muscles tensed. What if he died without Bryan being able to tell Sam how much he loved him? Sam had been in surgery all night. Who knew how many blood transfusions he'd been given at this point?

The doctors hadn't told them much, just that his injuries were extensive and they would do everything they could. What did *everything they could* mean? It was hopeless? Sam was only twenty-five years old. His entire life was ahead of him.

Sam could not die.

Bryan's blood simmered in his veins. How could this be happening? He jerked his coffee cup too quickly, and it spilled on the table.

Like an automaton, Libby swiped it with a napkin. Bags hung low under Tommy's eyes, and each of them fidgeted in their own way. Libby yanked on a lock of hair near her shoulder. Tommy drummed the tabletop with his fingers and rapped it with his knuckles twice before raking his hand through his hair and repeating the process. And Bryan picked up his cup, set it back down, picked it up again. He wanted to hurl it at the wall as hard as he could.

"Do you think they've heard anything?" Libby asked in a tiny voice, a dot of hope lighting her eyes. "Should I text Jake?"

"Dad would have called us." Tommy shoved his hand through his hair again. "You want to go back up? Or I can get Jake if you need him."

"No, all I do is fall apart up there. I think Jake needs a break from my tears as much as I do." She tried to smile, but her face fell, and Bryan's heart bunched up for her. She and Sam were close in age, and they'd always shared a special bond.

"Thankfully, Jeremy is a strong swimmer," Tommy said. "How in the world did he drag Sam to shore when his own leg was gashed open? Has anyone checked on him in a while?"

"He was sleeping," Libby said. "And they wouldn't let anyone see him but family the last time we checked."

Bryan tapped his fist against his chin. "I should have

gone on the boat with him and Jeremy. They asked me to, but I..."

"Don't, Bryan." Libby covered his hand with hers. "Even if you had been on the boat, you couldn't have stopped the accident. It's hard enough having Sam in there. What if you had been hurt, too?" A fresh batch of tears slid down her cheeks.

Bryan leaned over and rubbed her back. "It's okay. He's going to be okay."

"He lost a lot of blood, Bryan. His chances aren't good."

Tommy rapped his knuckles on the table. "What I don't get is how the speedboat didn't see them. How could it have plowed right into Granddad's fishing boat head-on? I want an investigation. If the sheriff doesn't call me back, I'm calling him."

"The sheriff is doing a full investigation. You know that. Dad's been on the phone with him all night." Bryan picked up his cup. Set it down.

He had the most incredible urge to see Jade. Her presence always made him feel stronger, better. Without her, he'd gone back to feeling helpless. He didn't want to imagine his days without her in them. But if he called her now, he'd blurt out everything, and what if she didn't believe him? Or worse, told him it was his grief talking?

She was the best friend he'd ever had.

She would know the right thing to say to soothe this black hole of emotions.

A text dinged for Tommy. "I'll be back. I'm calling Stephanie." He stalked away.

"Have you called Jade?" Libby asked.

He shook his head, keeping his gaze on his coffee.

"I'll call her." Libby picked up her phone. "She always knows what to say. I feel so lost right now."

"Wait." Bryan touched her wrist. "Can you not call her?"

"Why?" Libby swiped her finger on the phone. "What's going on?"

"Nothing. Well, something. But I need to think it through."

"Think what through?"

"I like her, Libby."

"Duh." Libby set the phone down. "So why don't you call her?"

Bryan let out a deep breath. "I messed things up yesterday, and I don't want to make it worse."

"Messed up how?"

Heat climbed his neck. He yanked his collar. "That's not important."

"You kissed her, didn't you?"

He concentrated on his coffee cup.

"What's the problem?" Libby asked. "She likes you."

"I don't know."

"Bryan, just because she's nervous doesn't mean she's not into you."

"Let's drop it. We have more important things to think about."

"I'm not dropping it. She's one of my best friends…"

He snorted.

"What? You don't think we're friends?"

"Libby, I know you're friends, and that's why I don't want you to call her right now. I'm not ready."

"What does me calling her have to do with you being ready?"

"I need to think before I talk to her." He gripped the foam cup. "I don't want to blow it with her."

"You might have a point." Libby nodded. "Has she told you about her mom? How her grandma raised her?"

He nodded.

"Yeah, me, too." Libby bit her lower lip. "A couple weeks ago I couldn't sleep, and I started putting myself in her shoes. Moving to a strange town with no family around. And I thought, well, I'd have my family in Lake Endwell. But it hit me Jade doesn't have that. She's nearly all alone in life."

Bryan nodded. "It's true."

"And moving here was a huge step for her. She's doing great at Shine Gifts, and everyone who meets her can't help but like her. She's got one of those personalities, you know, where you want to stay in the same room with her for as long as possible."

He did know. Everything Libby said, he hadn't been able to put into words.

"So I think you're right. You need to tread carefully. For her to take a chance on love is scary. She has a lot to lose if it doesn't work out. I've seen you two together. Her eyes light up whenever you're around. And she gravitates toward you."

He hoped so. Both their cell phones dinged. They met each other's eyes. Fear. Dread. They grabbed the phones and read the text from Dad.

Sam's out of surgery. Unconscious. Come up.

Jade slid the shirt out of the hot press and hung it on a hanger. The clock on the wall ticktocked to 5:16. The sun hadn't risen yet. She'd tossed and turned for hours last night until finally giving up and coming down here. Might as well fill a few orders before the store opened at ten. It was better than trying to make sense of the thoughts circling like buzzards in her head. She rubbed her eyes and pulled out a stool.

For the first time she hadn't gotten a thrill when she unlocked the store. She'd turned on the lights, sighed and trudged to the back. It was just a building. Lovely, useful, but it didn't hold her hand the way Bryan did.

Maybe being a backup plan was better than nothing. Could she really enjoy Lake Endwell without Bryan?

Folding her hands, she dropped her forehead. Weariness crushed her shoulders, but if she went back to bed now, she wouldn't sleep.

Lord, I'm having a hard time here.

Bryan's face flashed before her. The indecision in his eyes after their kiss.

He didn't love her. He liked her. They'd spent time together, enjoyed each other's company, but that didn't mean…

She wiped her forehead. That's exactly what spending time together and getting close meant—falling in love. Bryan might love her, but he was too afraid to take another chance. He'd said all along he wasn't dating or getting married. And she wanted both. She could have opened a store anywhere in the world, but she chose here because of Mimi's love story.

Grunting, she let her head drop. A guy like Bryan who'd been burned so badly before wouldn't put himself through rejection again.

Jade rubbed her forearms and shivered. *Lord, why is love so hard? I want to trust You have blessings for me, the way Mimi always said, but all I really want is Bryan.*

Exhaustion hit her. Grabbing a tissue, she blew her nose.

Liar. If all she wanted was Bryan, why was she putting Lake Endwell first? Wouldn't she be willing to meet him halfway? Or all the way? Maybe Lake Endwell was a stepping stone to her dreams coming true. Mimi and Poppi made a life for themselves in Las Vegas.

What was more important?

Lake Endwell? Or Bryan?

Chapter Fifteen

Bryan waited with his family as each of them took turns going into Sam's room in the ICU. Dad had been the first to see Sam after the doctors gave him the okay. The propeller from the other boat's motor had lacerated the length of Sam's right side. The doctors were able to sew him up, but the propeller had also sliced through tendons in his thigh. Two ribs were broken, and they'd given him blood transfusions throughout the night. There was a slim chance of brain damage, but they wouldn't know for sure until Sam regained consciousness.

The doctors made it clear Sam was not out of the danger zone yet. Even if he pulled through the way they hoped, he would need physical therapy for months. He might never be able to use his right leg again.

Bryan was still trying to wrap his head around it. He'd taken his brother's presence for granted. Couldn't imagine life without him.

Claire came out of Sam's room and burst into tears. Reed drew her in his arms tightly and kissed the top of her head. Libby and Jake huddled together on a couch, and Uncle Joe kept an arm around Aunt Sally, who had a blank look in her eyes. He'd never seen his family so shell-shocked.

"Your turn." Dad, his face ashen and slack as if he'd aged ten years, nodded at Bryan. "Has anyone called his assistant manager? She needs to know what's going on. You might have to help out with his dealership the next couple of months."

"Anything, Dad," Bryan said, his throat full of sand. "Anything he needs."

Dad put his hand on Bryan's shoulder, then pulled him in for a hug. Sensing his devastation, Bryan held him a minute and whispered, "I'm praying."

Dad stepped back, quickly wiping under his eyes. "We have a good Lord. He will get us through no matter what."

Bryan slipped into Sam's room. At the sight of his brother wrapped in bandages with tubes sticking out everywhere, his face as white as the blanket around his legs, Bryan dropped to the chair next to his bed and couldn't control his emotions any longer.

Why him, God? Why my little brother? He has so much to live for. Why did he have to go through this?

He took Sam's hand in his. If only Sam would wake up, tease him about something—even get mad about the dumb dog. Bryan squeezed his eyes shut as tears streamed down his face. Sobs silently shook his shoulders.

"I'd take your place in a minute, Sam. I hate that this happened to you." He lifted Sam's hand and held it between both of his. Kissed Sam's knuckles. "I love you. I can't lose you, brother, not now. You've got to fight. Fight for me. Fight for all of us."

We're not given all the time in the world, are we? I should have made more of an effort with him. I wasted precious time.

At least he and Sam had cleared the air the other night. Their heart-to-heart had left them closer than they'd ever been. But Bryan still couldn't help thinking he should have gone on the boat. Should have been with him and Jeremy. Maybe he could have prevented the accident. Protected them.

A nurse entered the room and discreetly checked Sam's vitals. Bryan stood, found a tissue and cleaned himself up as best he could. He turned to the nurse. "Is this normal?"

The nurse gently steered him to the door. "The fact he made it through surgery is a good sign. He'll probably go in and out of being awake all day. He needs rest. You look like you could use some, too. Go home, get some sleep and come back later."

When Bryan stepped into the hallway, he had to force his body upright to keep it from sliding to the floor.

"I spoke with the doctor." Dad looked him in the eye. "They aren't allowing any of us in there again until this afternoon. Why don't you go home. I'll call you the second I hear anything. All night they've been telling us to get some rest. I think you need it."

"What about you?" The set of Dad's jaw told Bryan he was there for the long haul.

"I'll hunker down on a couch for a while."

Bryan glanced over at his family and didn't have it in him to tell them goodbye. His emotions crushed him. Before he lost it again, he strode to the elevator and escaped.

The elevator opened on the main floor, and he made his way down the hall to the exit. He emerged outside as the sun began to rise. He stopped short.

God, I couldn't have done anything to prevent this, could I? The speedboat still would have hit them. And I

*couldn't have stopped Abby from cheating on me, either.
She wasn't committed to me.*

It was time to accept God made him who he was for
a reason. Uncomplicated. Protective. And he wouldn't
have it any other way.

"Jade, I'm sorry to call so early, but have you seen
Bryan?" Libby's voice sounded distraught over the phone.
Early for Libby to be calling. Jade checked the clock—
7:12.

"I saw him yesterday afternoon, why?" A shiver raced
down Jade's back. She didn't want to tell her about what
happened in case Libby got mad at her, but she desper-
ately wanted to confide in someone. Jade tossed the tote
bag she was getting ready to decal on the counter.

"Sam was in an accident," Libby said, her voice catching. "We've been at the hospital all night, but Bryan left
a few hours ago and none of us has seen him since. He's
not returning our texts."

"Oh, no! What happened?" Jade clapped her hand over
her chest. Sam's merry eyes and infectious laugh came
to mind. *Not Sam.*

"Around five thirty last night a speedboat crashed
into the fishing boat he and his friend were on." Libby
started crying.

"How badly was he injured? Please tell me he's going
to be okay." She ached to hug Libby.

"It's bad, Jade. He was in surgery all night. A propeller
tore his right side up. They gave him blood transfusions..."
Libby's soft cries came in waves. "He might not walk again."

"I'm so sorry," Jade said quietly. "What can I do?"

She sniffed a few times and drew in a loud breath.
"There's nothing we can do at this point except pray. Sam
briefly regained consciousness, but the doctors won't let

any of us see him again until later. I was hoping you knew where Bryan was. When he came out of Sam's room… I've never seen him look like that."

Jade's heart clenched, and she could barely breathe. "I'll try to find him, Libby."

"None of us want to leave the hospital right now. Dad said Bryan's fine, and Claire told me to let him deal with this on his own, but I've got a bad feeling."

Jade had a bad feeling, too. "You hang tight. I'll do my best to find him and keep you posted. And I'm praying for you all, especially Sam."

"Thanks, Jade."

They hung up, and Jade pressed her palms against the counter to steady herself. How could this have happened? Yesterday Sam had waved to her in church. And now? She willed the threatening tears away. She couldn't indulge in a breakdown. Not when Bryan was out there suffering.

Bryan. Strong, quiet Bryan. A rip tore down her heart. She'd hurt him yesterday, and then he'd found out about Sam… She choked on a cry. He and Sam seemed so close, the way they teased each other. What must Bryan be thinking?

And where was he?

She tossed her phone in her purse, scribbled a quick note—Shine Gifts Won't Be Open Today—taped it to the door and raced to her little car. She'd check his house first.

The three-minute drive took a lifetime. Her brain filled with fears, regrets and sympathy. His truck wasn't in his driveway, but she knocked on the front door, anyway. No answer.

What now?

She sat on the porch step with her head in her hands. Where could he be? Where would he go?

Please God, don't fail me now. Help me find him.

Jade marched around the house and stopped short. Teeny wasn't in her fenced dog run. Bryan told her he never left the dog alone in the house. Unless he'd been too upset when he left last night. Entirely possible.

She peeked in the front windows. No sign of Teeny.

Bryan had to be worried sick about Sam. Where would he go in a situation like this?

She leaned her forehead against the window. *Where? Think!*

It hit her. She knew exactly where Bryan was.

Granddad's camping spot.

The thought of him in pain by himself in the middle of nowhere pierced her right through the soul.

She would not let him go through this alone.

Jade ran back to her car and drove to her apartment. After throwing two water bottles, a handful of bagged snacks, a compass, a Swiss Army knife, her phone and the small emergency kit she'd prepared last week into a backpack, she scurried to her bedroom to change into jeans and hiking boots. She inhaled, counted to three and left.

He needed her. She could do this.

Ten minutes later she spotted his truck on old Ranger Road. She parked behind it and ran through a mental checklist. Would she remember how to get there? She'd entered the exact location into her GPS watch last week when she and Bryan packed the blanket to go home. One way or another, she would find him.

Marching along the edge of the bean field, she made good time and found herself at the woods where the path started. She stared up, up, up at the trees. The sun was bright. It promised to be a hot day.

She took a moment to get centered. She'd never hiked in the woods by herself. Her throat prickled. Familiar, unwanted sensations flitted in and out—of chasing after the boys, of clutching her puppy, of wandering for hours, tears streaking down her face, crying out for help.

Lord, I'm not seven anymore, and this isn't Germany. Bryan is in there. He's hurting, alone and possibly scared. I need You to get me through this forest. I need You to keep me strong.

Jade lifted her chin and stepped out of the light into the woods. The first twenty yards were fine. But the trees grew closer together, and as she kept moving, her head started to spin.

Not now! She couldn't have a panic attack. She had to think of Bryan. Tears fell one by one, but she pressed forward. A little crying wouldn't stop her.

A huge black bird swooped in front of her, and she gasped, blood pumping hard through her veins. Where had that thing come from?

She shook her head. Stomped all the way to the curve up ahead. Birch trees and ferns had taken over this area, and her spirits lifted. *Not everything out here is scary.*

The longer she hiked, the more she became lost in her thoughts.

God had led her to Lake Endwell. For a store, yes, but for more. He'd led her on this path—this scary wooded path—the way Mimi always promised her He would. Jade had never guessed Mimi meant a literal path.

The path led to Bryan.

"I trust You, God," she whispered. A squirrel scurried in front of her, stopped, looked at her and went on his frenzied way. She let out a shaky laugh. "I trust You!"

She found the stream. The log over it appeared slippery, but she crossed it with ease. The clearing was mere yards away. Her heartbeat sped up in excitement. She'd made it! All by herself!

Not all by herself. She'd made it with God's help.

I've never been alone, have I? God, You were with me during those terrifying hours in Germany. You've always been with me.

Joy filled her soul, followed by peace. She could have died that summer, but God had sent someone to find her. He hadn't neglected her. He'd protected her. Saved her. She wanted to weep in gratitude.

But she had a mission to finish.

Bryan needed her.

She ran the rest of the way.

Bryan sat next to Teeny on the thin blanket he'd shoved into his backpack. Legs pulled up, forearms resting on his knees, he looked out at the expanse of blue sky. He'd been at Granddad's spot for over an hour, and he'd been praying hard. He prayed for Sam to heal completely. For their family to be comforted while they waited, especially Dad.

His memories of this spot returned. Granddad with his walking stick, standing tall and proud right here, pointing at a hawk flying overhead. Special times. Ones Bryan treasured.

Felt like yesterday he'd hung on Granddad's every word. Back then, he trusted everything would work out when he got older. Bryan never imagined he'd be divorced or that Sam would be nearly killed.

Bryan mindlessly stroked Teeny's fur. Dad had texted him an hour ago. Sam regained consciousness briefly.

Poor Sam had a rough road ahead of him. Healing would be a long and painful process.

He should get back to the hospital. But something held him back.

Tommy's words from the other night whispered in his head. *Do you believe you're divinely guided? You'll always take the right turn in the road.*

Marrying Abby had felt like a wrong turn, but if he hadn't married her, he would have married someone else. Right this minute he could be at the hospital with a different wife and family. But he'd be married to the wrong woman. He'd be part of the wrong family.

Anyone but Jade was wrong for him.

Jade was his right turn in the road.

He and Jade belonged together. God had brought her to Lake Endwell. Whatever their future, Bryan was meant to fall in love with her. She'd healed him. Made him finally grasp he could have a full life with a love of his own.

Life was delicate, short.

Too short to live alone when he had a brave, beautiful, light-up-the-room woman. Libby was right. Jade had family baggage. He'd known it from day one. And he wanted to take those bags out of her hands and help her carry them.

He just needed to convince her to let him.

A rustling sound came from the tree line. He strained his neck to see what was causing it. *No.* It couldn't be.

Jade ran through the wildflowers and grass. He unfolded his legs and jumped up as she threw herself in his arms. He gladly caught her, lifting her off her feet and holding her tightly.

"Whoa. How did you…? Why are you…?" He set her down. It was as if a floodlight lit his soul. Teeny sat up, licked Jade's hand and flopped back on the blanket.

"Oh, Bryan, when Libby called so worried, I promised her I'd find you. And I drove to your house, but you weren't there, and I didn't see Teeny, and I knew. I knew you had to have come here. I couldn't let you be out here by yourself. My heart couldn't bear to think of you alone."

"Slow down," he said in a low voice. She'd come for him. She'd worried about him. She'd… "You hiked out here all by yourself?"

She nodded.

"You were that worried about me?"

Biting her lip, she nodded again.

The full impact of what she'd done for him landed in his gut. She'd willingly hiked by herself for miles through woods so he wouldn't be alone. She—who'd trembled in fear at the sight of trees mere weeks ago and still gripped his hand when they trekked through wooded areas—had braved her way through a forest she'd only been to once?

He tried to comprehend it. He couldn't. *She did that for me?*

"How was it, Jade?" He cupped her cheek, caressing it with his thumb, and searched her eyes. They filled with tears.

"Pretty scary, but God was with me every step of the way." She nestled her cheek against his palm. "He's always been with me, even all those years ago. I just didn't understand that until now."

He struggled to find the words he wanted to say, but they eluded him. "I'm glad you realized it."

"I am, too," she whispered. "I realized something else, Bryan. I haven't ever wanted to be your friend."

His heart lurched. Had he been wrong all along?

If she told him they had no future, what would he do?

I'll fight tooth and nail for her.

Jade lifted watery green eyes. "I've always wanted more than friendship with you from the day we met. When you told me about your wife, I was disappointed. Then I found out you weren't married, and I knew you were too good to be true. Honest. Dependable. You had integrity. I couldn't wrap my head around the fact a fascinating guy like you would ever stay interested in me."

His tongue stuck to his parched mouth. She thought all that? "I had to work through some scars from the divorce. I couldn't imagine you'd want me. And if you did, you'd figure out I'm not very exciting and you'd leave."

"You're exciting. You have so much knowledge up in your brain, and you make it sound so interesting. I love spending time with you." Smiling, she brushed her fingers across the hair above his forehead. "I moved to Lake Endwell on the hope of a dream. And I found you. If moving to Canada is still your plan, we'll make it work. Maybe Blue Mountain needs a T-shirt shop."

"Lake Endwell needs a T-shirt shop." The expression in his eyes seared her. Jade held her breath as Bryan shook his head. "I'm not moving."

"I'm not making you stay," she said. "You worked so hard for this."

"But I don't want it. Not really. I was escaping. I don't want to move, not if you're willing to take a chance on me."

"I love you, Bryan. I've been waiting for you all my life. I needed someone patient. Someone who didn't think less of me because I was absolutely petrified of trees. And there you were. Teaching a survival class."

"You were my only student for a reason."

"God put us together."

"He did." Bryan trailed his hands down her biceps. "Last night I did a lot of thinking and praying."

Jade shivered. "I haven't asked how you're handling Sam's accident. Tell me everything."

"It's okay, Jade. Dad texted me an hour ago that Sam regained consciousness but is out again."

"Libby told me that, too." She took his hand and led him to sit next to her on the blanket where Teeny had fallen back to sleep. "Let me text Libby quick and let her know where you are. She was really worried."

After she finished, she turned her attention back to Bryan.

"I was so scared we'd lose him," Bryan said. "He and I had an argument, and afterward, we bonded—really bonded. I wasted a lifetime with him, Jade. I wasted it."

She slid her arm around his waist and rested her cheek against his shoulder. "No, you didn't. You two have always been close. Anyone can see it. The way you tease each other. You're comfortable with each other."

He turned his head to look at her. "You think so?"

"Yeah. I do. You've always loved him."

"No question."

"And he's always loved you."

"Absolutely."

She smiled. "Then there hasn't been any wasted time."

"Maybe." He stared ahead again. "But it made me realize I don't want to waste a minute not showing the people I love how I feel."

"You show it every day. You're the only person who I can say with absolute certainty would drop anything to help me."

"That's because I love you." He shifted, tilting her chin up with his thumb.

Her heart might burst if he kept looking at her like

that. He lowered his lips to hers. The kiss was a whisper, a promise.

"Yesterday—can it really have been less than twenty-four hours ago?" He hung his head. "You asked if you were my backup plan. You could never be anything but first in my life. I love you."

A thrill of anticipation rushed to her head.

"When I came out of Sam's room, I didn't know if I could even stand up. The thought of losing him crushed me."

Her throat swelled with emotion. The thought crushed her, too, and Sam wasn't even her brother.

"And I looked around and saw Claire clutching Reed, and Libby leaning on Jake, and all I could think was how much I needed you there. You'd know what to say. You have this way about you, this ease. You comfort me, challenge me, bring out the best in me." He caressed her cheek. "I'm not great with words. I'm not doing this right, but my heart is yours. All you have to do is claim it. I love you. I want forever with you, Jade."

She couldn't breathe. Had she heard him correctly? "I love you, too. I'm claiming it, Bryan. You've had my heart all along." She threw her arms around his neck. "You're my best friend, and I can't imagine a day without you."

"I don't want to imagine a day without you. You're everything to me."

He kissed her. She tasted commitment and a lifetime of joy. They held each other, in no rush to do anything but stay. When Bryan held his hand out to help her up, she pressed her lips to it before rising.

"Let's see how Sam is doing," he said.

"Are you sure you want me with you?" She took

Teeny's leash and stooped to pet her. The dog licked her face.

"I'm not going without you. I need you there, Jade. It's hard."

She twined her arm through his. "Then I won't leave your side."

"Bryan! Jade!" Libby pulled them both into a hug. "He doesn't have brain damage!"

Bryan thrust his hand against the wall. *Praise God!* "You're sure? There's none?"

The dark circles under Libby's eyes didn't mask her joy as she nodded. "The doctor let Dad go in for a minute, but Sam needs rest. They won't let anyone else in until tonight. We're all heading home to get some sleep."

"Is there anything I can do, Libby?" Jade held both of Libby's hands in hers.

Libby shook her head. "Thank you for everything." She turned to Bryan, punching his arm. "You scared me. Why didn't you tell us where you were going?"

"I needed to be alone." He smiled. "But it makes me feel good you were worried about me."

"Of course I worried about you. You're my big brother."

Bryan kissed her cheek. "I worry about you, too, Libs."

"Don't make me start crying again." She tapped her fingertips under her eyes as Jake approached and put his arm around her.

"Let's get you home," Jake said. He led her down the hall.

Bryan spotted Dad. "Just a minute, Jade. I want to make sure he's doing okay."

"I'll see how Sally's doing. Take your time."

Bryan crossed to the hallway where Dad had been talking to a nurse. "How are you holding up?"

He let his breath expand his cheeks before exhaling. "Better. Did they tell you there isn't any brain damage?"

"Yeah." Bryan took his arm. "Come on. Let's sit down. You look beat."

His energetic father could barely stand. Bryan tightened his hold. He settled him into a chair and sat in the one next to him.

"I lost your mother. Thought that was the worst day of my life. But losing one of you kids?" Dad buried his head in his hands and his shoulders shook. Bryan had never seen him cry, and it tore at his heart to hear those gut-wrenching sobs.

He rubbed Dad's back. "It's okay. You don't have to hold it in. We'll be here for Sam. We're not going to lose him."

Dad nodded, wiping his face. "I know. I know. I just... couldn't let myself feel anything until..."

"You knew for sure."

"Yeah."

Bryan pulled him into an embrace. "It's been an awful night. We all need some sleep."

Dad straightened, rubbing his bloodshot eyes. "I couldn't agree more. I'm going home."

"Let me drive you."

Aunt Sally, Uncle Joe and Jade approached.

"Come on, Dale, you're coming home with us. I'm tucking you into the guest room."

Dad opened his mouth to protest, then nodded. "That sounds good. I don't know if I could sleep at home."

Uncle Joe took Bryan aside. "Don't worry. We'll take care of him."

"I know you will. Thanks."

Bryan slung his arm over Jade's shoulders. Out in the parking lot, he helped her into his truck.

They drove in easy silence until they reached Lake Endwell's city limits.

"This isn't the way. My car's still parked on old Ranger Road." Jade looked out her window and frowned at him.

"I have something I need to do."

"You're exhausted. You need to sleep."

"Not yet." He drove down Main Street and cut the engine in City Park's lot. "Come on."

"Why are we here?"

"You'll see."

He held her hand tightly, leading her to the beech tree near the gazebo. When they reached it, he slid a pocketknife out and grinned.

"Are you doing what I think you're doing?" Her eyes sparkled as brilliant as the lake beyond them.

"What do you think I'm doing?"

"Carving? Initials?" Her voice sounded small, hopeful.

"I am."

"Really?"

Right next to Frank and Mimi's initials, he carved *J & B* and circled it with a heart.

"Really. I want the whole world to know I love you, Jade Emerson."

Jade twined her arms around his waist and looked up into his eyes. "You're mine and I'm never letting you go."

Epilogue

"Are you finally going to tell me where you two are going on your honeymoon?"

Jade adjusted her train and checked her veil. She and Libby stood in the restroom of Uncle Joe's Restaurant. The wedding had been perfect. Claire and Libby had helped coordinate all the details. From the walk up the aisle in the flower-filled church to the delicious reception dinner right here. Both sets of her parents had even made the trip.

"I guess it's okay to spill it now." Jade applied another coat of raspberry lipstick, puckered her lips and grinned. "Since I'm not afraid of trees anymore, we're hiking through the Black Forest."

Libby's face fell in horror. "You are not."

"I'm teasing." Jade laughed, picking up her train. "We're not."

"For a minute there, I thought you were serious." Libby held the door open to go back out to the dining hall. "So where are you really going?"

"I booked the honeymoon suite at a resort in Blue Mountain, Ontario."

"Have I thanked you enough for preventing him from

going on that interview? I still can't believe he actually considered moving away from us all." The band launched into a country song as Libby and Jade sidestepped two kids running toward the cake table. "I was sure you were taking him to Las Vegas. Figured you'd want to show him your hometown."

"Oh, I have that trip planned for later in the year." Jade winked. "I'll slip a tour of the Grand Canyon in for giggles."

"Something tells me Bryan will love the Grand Canyon." They strolled to the head table. "Who's watching Teeny?"

"Dale. He's got a soft spot for the mutt." Jade still couldn't believe they'd been able to adopt the dog from Lucy. She'd been offered a job in Spain after graduating and agreed Teeny would be happy with Jade and Bryan. They still texted Lucy photos now and then.

"Thanks for being my matron of honor, Libby."

"Thank you." Libby hugged her. "I'm honored you asked. I'm going to text Sam and see how he's doing."

Sam, in a wheelchair, had been a groomsman at the ceremony but had skipped the reception to rest. It had been five months since the accident, and his recovery was slow and ongoing. The rest of the Sheffield siblings mingled in their bridesmaids' dresses and tuxedos, and Macy was particularly sweet in her flower-girl dress. She'd bounced up the aisle, spreading rose pedals with glee. Stephanie and Tom's baby, Emily, whom everyone called Sweetpea, was home with a babysitter.

"Ah, there's my bride." Bryan appeared next to Jade. "How are you doing, Mrs. Sheffield?" His breath warmed Jade's cheek as he pulled her to him.

"Couldn't be better." Her breath caught at how handsome he looked. And here she'd thought all the good ones were taken. God had saved the best for her. Mimi would approve. "How about you? You look as though you have a secret."

"Me? No." He whisked her across the room to the patio doors. Autumn leaves covered the deck, but he led her outside. "Have I told you how beautiful you are?"

"Yes." She grinned. He pressed his lips to hers. Her husband. Joy filled her heart. She tweaked his tie. "Tell me again."

"You're beautiful. You're mine. And I'm yours." He rested his forehead against hers. Mischief danced in his eyes as he pulled something out of his pocket and handed it to her. "You might need this."

"A paper bag?" She snatched it out of his hand and scrunched her nose. "And why would I need it?"

"You'll see." He bent his head to kiss her, but she ducked, laughing.

She arched her eyebrows and drew herself up to full height. "I hope you know what you're doing."

"I know what I'm doing." He tossed the paper bag over his shoulder and kissed her thoroughly.

"Grab the paper bag." She pretended to fan herself. "I might need it if you keep kissing me like that."

"Anything for you."

* * * * *

Dear Reader,

I'm so thankful for the chance to write Bryan's story. Failed relationships can emotionally scar the strongest person. God graciously sends people in our path just when we need them the most. I can't tell you how many times I've received a letter or bumped into a friend when I was at a low point. Those small gestures—a smile, a hug, a kind word—can make all the difference in a person's day.

Bryan was ready to give up on his deepest dream of having a wife and family, but then Jade arrived. She needed help only he could offer, and she, in turn, brought him friendship and hope. I pray you will always be blessed by someone and will offer comfort when you see a need. Never be afraid to pray for God's guidance. He'll be with you every step of the way.

I love connecting with readers. Please stop by my website, www.jillkemerer.com, and email me at jill@jillkemerer.com.

God bless you!
Jill Kemerer

REQUEST YOUR FREE BOOKS!

2 FREE INSPIRATIONAL NOVELS
PLUS 2
FREE
MYSTERY GIFTS

Love Inspired®

YES! Please send me 2 FREE Love Inspired® novels and my 2 FREE mystery gifts (gifts are worth about \$10). After receiving them, if I don't wish to receive any more books, I can return the shipping statement marked "cancel." If I don't cancel, I will receive 6 brand-new novels every month and be billed just \$4.99 per book in the U.S. or \$5.49 per book in Canada. That's a saving of at least 17% off the cover price. It's quite a bargain! Shipping and handling is just 50¢ per book in the U.S. and 75¢ per book in Canada.* I understand that accepting the 2 free books and gifts places me under no obligation to buy anything. I can always return a shipment and cancel at any time. Even if I never buy another book, the two free books and gifts are mine to keep forever.

105/305 IDN GH5P

Name _____ (PLEASE PRINT) _____

Address _____ Apt. # _____

City _____ State/Prov. _____ Zip/Postal Code _____

Signature (if under 18, a parent or guardian must sign)

Mail to the **Reader Service:**
IN U.S.A.: P.O. Box 1867, Buffalo, NY 14240-1867
IN CANADA: P.O. Box 609, Fort Erie, Ontario L2A 5X3

**Are you a subscriber to Love Inspired® books
and want to receive the larger-print edition?
Call 1-800-873-8635 or visit www.ReaderService.com.**

* Terms and prices subject to change without notice. Prices do not include applicable taxes. Sales tax applicable in N.Y. Canadian residents will be charged applicable taxes. Offer not valid in Quebec. This offer is limited to one order per household. Not valid for current subscribers to Love Inspired books. All orders subject to credit approval. Credit or debit balances in a customer's account(s) may be offset by any other outstanding balance owed by or to the customer. Please allow 4 to 6 weeks for delivery. Offer available while quantities last.

Your Privacy—The Reader Service is committed to protecting your privacy. Our Privacy Policy is available online at www.ReaderService.com or upon request from the Reader Service.

We make a portion of our mailing list available to reputable third parties that offer products we believe may interest you. If you prefer that we not exchange your name with third parties, or if you wish to clarify or modify your communication preferences, please visit us at www.ReaderService.com/consumerchoice or write to us at Reader Service Preference Service, P.O. Box 9062, Buffalo, NY 14240-9062. Include your complete name and address.

LI15

"Will you give me an answer, Rebekah? Will you marry me?"

"But why? I don't love you." Her cheeks turned to fire as she hurried to add, "That sounded awful. I'm sorry. The truth is you've always been a *gut* friend, Joshua, which is why I feel I can be blunt."

"If we can't speak honestly now, I can't imagine when we could."

"Then I will honestly say I don't understand why you'd ask me to m-m-marry you." She hated how she stumbled over the simple word.

No, it wasn't simple. There was nothing simple about Joshua Stoltzfus appearing at her door to ask her to become his wife.

"Because we could help each other. Isn't that what a husband and wife are? Helpmeets?" He cleared his throat. "I would rather marry a woman I know and respect as a friend. We've both married once for love, and we've both lost the ones we love. Is it wrong to be more practical this time?"

Every inch of her wanted to shout, *"Ja!"* But his words made sense.

She had married Lloyd because she'd been infatuated with him and the idea of being his wife, so much so that she had convinced herself while they were courting to ignore how rough and demanding he had been with her when she'd caught the odor of beer on his breath. She'd accepted his excuses and his reassurances it wouldn't happen again…even when it had. She'd been blinded by love. How much better would it be to marry with her eyes wide-open? No surprises, and a husband whom she counted among her friends.

She'd be a fool not to agree immediately. "All right," she said. "I will marry you."

"Really?" He appeared shocked, as if he hadn't thought she'd agree quickly.

"Ja." She didn't add anything more, because there wasn't anything more to say. They would be wed, for better or for worse. And she was sure the worse couldn't be as bad as her marriage to Lloyd.

Don't miss
AN AMISH MATCH
by Jo Ann Brown,
available May 2016 wherever
Love Inspired® books and ebooks are sold.

www.LoveInspired.com

SPECIAL EXCERPT FROM

Love Inspired **HISTORICAL**

*Town founder Will Canfield has big dreams for
Cowboy Creek—but his plans are thrown for a loop
when a tiny bundle is left on his doorstep. With a
baby to care for, the last thing he needs is another
complication. But that's just what he gets, in the form
of a redheaded, trouble-making cowgirl who throws his
world upside down.*

Read on for a sneak preview of
Sherri Shackelford's
SPECIAL DELIVERY BABY,
the exciting continuation of the miniseries
COWBOY CREEK,
available May 2016 from Love Inspired Historical.

"The name is Will Canfield," he said. "Thank you for
your assistance, Miss Stone."

"You sure picked a dangerous place to take your baby
for a walk, Daddy Canfield. Might want to reconsider
your route next time."

The measured expression on his face faltered a notch.
"Oh, this isn't my baby."

She hoisted an eyebrow. "Reckon who that baby
belongs to is none of my business one way or the other."
She gestured toward the child. "I think your girl is getting
hungry. Better get mama."

"That's the whole problem." The man spoke more to
the infant in his arms than to her. "Someone abandoned
her. I found her on my doorstep just now." He glanced
over his shoulder and then back at her. "The woman—
the one who spooked the cattle. Did you see which way

she ran? I think this child belongs to her. If not, then she might have seen something. She was hiding in the shadows when I discovered this little bundle."

"Sorry. I was focused on the cattle."

Clearly frustrated by her answers, Daddy Canfield muttered something unintelligible.

He grimaced and held the bundle away from him, revealing a dark, wet patch on his expensive suit coat.

Tomasina chuckled. The boys were going to love hearing about this one. They'd never believe her but they'd love the telling. Her pa always liked a good yarn, as well. At the thought of her pa, her smile faded. He'd died on the trail a few weeks back and they'd buried him in Oklahoma Territory. The wound of his loss was still raw and she shied away from her memories of him.

"Fellow…" Tomasina said. "As much fun as this has been, I'd best be getting on."

"Thanks for your help back there," Will replied, his tone grudging. "Your quick action averted a disaster."

The admission had obviously cost him. He struck her as a prideful man, and prideful men sometimes needed a reminder of their place in the grand scheme of things.

"Daddy Canfield," she declared. "Since you don't like guns, how do you feel about rodeo shows? You know, trick riding and fancy target shooting?"

"Not in my town. Too dangerous."

"Excellent," Tomasina replied with a hearty grin.

Yep. She felt better already.

Don't miss SPECIAL DELIVERY BABY
by Sherri Shackelford,
available May 2016 wherever
Love Inspired® Historical books and ebooks are sold.
www.LoveInspired.com